# RICHARD ALLEN
## SKINHEAD

Richard Allen was the pen-name of James Moffat, born in Canada in 1922.

Moffat was prolific, though one repeated claim that he was the author of 'at least 290 novels in several genres under at least 45 pseudonyms' still requires independent verification. It is known that Moffat contributed to an early draft of the novel *Somewhere in The Night*, which was later completed (or entirely rewritten – sources differ) by Michael Moorcock and published under the pseudonym Bill Barclay in 1966.

However it was Moffat's gritty youthsploitation novels, all written in the 1970's under the name Richard Allen, that form the bulk of his legacy today. The Joe Hawkins story began in *Skinhead* (1970) and was continued in *Suedehead* (1971). Later there were further instalments in Joe Hawkins' story, as well as novels focussing on other youth movements such as *Smoothies* (1973), *Punk Rock* (1977) and the final Allen novel *Mod Rule* (1980). Altogether there were eighteen novels under the Richard Allen brand.

James Moffat spent most of his final decade in obscurity, though he lived to see the reissue of the Richard Allen novels in the early 1990's. He died in July of 1993, while living in a nursing home in Newton Abbot.

**Also by Richard Allen**

Suedehead

# RICHARD ALLEN

## SKINHEAD

With an introduction
by Andrew Stevens

DEAN STREET PRESS

Published by Dean Street Press 2015

Copyright © 1970 Richard Allen

All Rights Reserved

Published by licence, issued under the UK Orphan Works
Licensing Scheme

First published in 1970 by New English Library

Cover by DSP

ISBN 978 1 911095 41 5

www.deanstreetpress.co.uk

# INTRODUCTION

RICHARD ALLEN'S *Skinhead* (1970) was the first instalment of a cycle of pulp novels (since described as "paperback nasties" by John Harrison) which firmly established the New English Library as entirely symbolic of the era in which they were rooted and the passing fad nature of youth cults.

*Skinhead* is brilliantly evocative of its time and place in early 1970s Plaistow, East London. The taut prose forms a concrete understanding of the milieu and mores of the post-Mod boots and braces culture of British working class youth and its social impact.

The first few *Skinhead* titles were published at a time when *Clockwork Orange* copycat violence was allegedly being meted out as quickly as municipal tower blocks and concrete car parks could be erected for it to take place in (a murder case of the time saw "sensational literature" cited in mitigation). Further dark episodes in the nation's psyche, such as the Black Panther murders, were not far behind.

Further evidence of the New English Library's (NEL's) former reputation is the reported existence of a Buckingham Palace Library-stamped copy of *Skinhead*, since the Queen's own interest was piqued by the ensuing tabloid outrage.

No passing seventies youth cult was spared the NEL treatment: bikers, punks, football hooligans and even Kung Fu. The *Skinhead* series was temporarily halted each time to take into account shifts in the zeitgeist, be it life on the long-haired campus left against a backdrop of Angry Brigade bombings and wider militancy (1971's *Demo*, a "masterfully-researched probe" according to its cover) or the latest manifestation of accelerated and manipulated teenybop (*Glam*, 1973).

The less-than-PC portrayal of *Skinhead*'s protagonist Joe Hawkins and his cohorts' acts of violence and rape, not to mention far from casual (but never organised) racism, in Richard Allen's work ("Richard Allen" was in fact an ageing hack by the name of James Moffat rather than the ear-to-the-ground bard of the terraces imagined by fans) cause many to blanch today. At the time these elements simply added to the series' allure and profitability.

In recent years discussion has shifted from Hawkins to Moffat himself; the image of a chain-smoking alcoholic hunched over a typewriter churning out opportunistic prose for a ready paycheque, almost an arresting and topic-worthy narrative in itself. There are tales of Moffat having to be locked in the NEL offices to meet a deadline, though the out-of-print cachet of the NEL titles tends towards furthering this mystique.

By the end of the cycle, 1980's *Mod Rule* (the protagonist Joe Hawkins' rape plot bastard offspring on this occasion, naturally), Moffat was understandably burnt out and NEL cut their losses accordingly – the imprint went on under a change of ownership in 1981 as a solidly mainstream thrillers and horrors concern.

As risible as the plots and violence became, parody and pastiche weren't far behind, affectionate or otherwise. Here we can count the satirical poise of artist Stewart Home, the best-selling Victor Headley of *Yardie* fame, not to mention the *Football Factory*'s John King's own *Skinheads* novel of 2008, the entire Attack! Books roster and the unabashed NEL stylings of *The Reprisalizer* (Warp Films, 2011).

In 1992 a timely reissue of Moffat's Richard Allen novels via *Skinhead Times* (featuring artwork in its own way as iconic as the earlier covers) recognised their cult status and global following. Far from being a passing fad, skinhead culture had gone through several iterations by this point, continuing to do so to this day.

Helpfully, the late Laurence James, an early editor at NEL and himself a pulp author as 'Mick Norman' (the writer behind NEL's aforementioned Hells Angels cash-ins) even then called them "nostalgia for a time when there really appeared to be 'no future'".

Andrew Stevens, May 2015

# SKINHEAD

# CHAPTER ONE

OUTSIDE THE SHED, a freighter blasted the lunch-hour silence with her whistle. The churn-churn of props frothed the Thames as a Liberian registered vessel slipped from her berth, holds battened down on the vital exports bound for South Africa.

Inside the shed, surrounded by an untidy clutter of unloaded merchandise, the dockers relaxed – sandwiches eaten, tea brewed and being sipped, the flick-flip of cards the only sound they wanted to hear.

Jack Boyle grinned across the upturned crate at his mate Roy. "Whatcha doin', Roy?"

Roy Hawkins studied his cards for the fourth time. He wasn't much of a poker player. Solo was more his game. "Blowed if I know, Jack."

Ed Black leant across Roy's shoulder and snorted disgustedly. "Pack 'er in, Roy," he offered. "Let me take your seat an' I'll show you 'ow the game should be played!"

Roy glanced at Jack and got a nodded agreement in return. Slowly, he replaced his coins inside his dirty overalls, carefully stacked his hand on the discard pile and relinquished his seat. He didn't mind. He had only taken a hand because Ed had to see a union representative at the gates. "What happened about the meeting?" Roy asked as Ed slumped into his place.

Ed set twenty quid on the table with a flourish. He fancied himself as *the* poker player of all time. His claim to fame was his ten hour visit to Las Vegas when sailing the P. & O. line to Vancouver and Japan. He never let his mates forget how he managed to sit in on a game with Red Skelton and come out showing a profit of six hundred dollars. What he forgot to mention was his subsequent call at a Gardena, California club and the loss of that six hundred plus every British penny he had in his pocket.

"Jack's got 'em by the short and curlies," he said loudly. "They got until Monday to meet our demands..."

"And then?" Roy asked, stuffing tobacco into his old briar.

Jack gathered the cards and started to shuffle the pack. His attention was focused on Ed but it didn't stop him doing an expert job and dealing five cards to each member of the school.

"Then we go out," Ed announced.

Roy scowled. He didn't like strikes. He believed in Jack Dash; believed in a working man's right to withdraw his labour for better pay. He didn't believe in frivolous disruptions of work – and, in his opinion, this latest episode was decidedly petty. "I'm against it Ed," he said.

Black spread his cards tight against his chest. He was a canny man; a distrusting individual. He studied the cards pointedly then, having proved his superiority, glanced leeringly at Roy. "You'll do exactly as Jack says!"

Roy nodded. *Yes*, he thought, *I'll follow the bloody band. I dare not go against it.* He believed that Jack Dash was the man closest to God; believed fervently in the right of the docker – and every working man – to take measures to combat the capitalistic employer. He was completely disenchanted with this Labour government – but he wouldn't abstain nor vote Tory. He would vote Labour as he always had; as his dad and his granddad had. It didn't matter what he said between elections – that the long period of Tory rule had been the best in living memory – providing that when the day came, he could make his "X" against the local Labour party candidate. In his constituency, Plaistow, the ineffectual hands on the helm of England counted for less than a man's worth to an employer. 1926 and the "cloth-cap" image had to be preserved. Forgotten were the affluent days of Tory rule. Forgotten were the massive debts piled on a staggering nation by yet another Labour administration. It didn't count that Britain was being dictated to by the International Monetary Fund.

"Are we playin' cards or discussin' the political situation?" Jack Boyle asked.

Ed Black glanced at his fellow-docker.

Roy smiled, puffing contentedly on his briar.

Solly Goldbluff smacked a fist into his palm and demanded, "Fuck the politicians and Jack Dash. I've got a hand – when are we goin' to play cards?"

Ed glared at Solly now, relinquished his platform to the determination showing on that Jewish face. He had never understood Solly; just as he had failed to appreciate Roy's hostility to the Labour movement as specified by extreme adherents like Dash. He knew that Roy would follow along in the main-stream of opinion; knew that Labour had an unswerving vote from Hawkins; knew too that the disenchantment Roy felt was common to the majority of trade unionists. Yet, he was assured by "cell" leaders, Roy and his mates would vote as usual when the crunch came.

Studying his cards, Ed shouted, "I'll open..."

Roy watched the game with lessened interest. He saw his mate win the pot; saw four other hefty hands go to Jack. Then, suddenly, it was time to return to work.

"It's a bleedin' shame," Jack Boyle said as they stepped outside the shed, "that Ed has it in for you, mate."

Hawkins shrugged and puffed on his pipe. "Oh, he isn't so bad."

"Like hell! He's a rotten bastard..." Jack's antagonism boiled over as Ed stepped from the shed with four of his special cronies trailing behind like bodyguards, ready to prevent physical harm to their adored leader. "Why don't you let Joe do him?"

Roy ignored Jack's suggestion. It was enough that he claimed fathership to the lad. He didn't have to be reminded what a rotten little bastard his son was nor to inflict him on one such as Ed Black. Basically, Roy was decent; law-abiding within the limits set by dockland. He did not consider pilfering a crime; it was a docker's perks to purloin Scotch and foodstuffs and the occasional costly items from "broken" packing cases. In the old days, Christmas would have been a barren table if it hadn't been for the goods stolen from the docks. Mostly, the employers and the police turned a blind-eye to the petty stealing. Only the capitalistic insurance concerns made a hue and cry about the extent of dockland thievery. Like so many of his mates, Roy didn't stop to consider that £10 a month taken from somebody else's pocket could multiply into a fantastic sum when set against the total number of dockers in the nation.

"'Owabout it, Roy?" Jack insisted.

"Forget Joe," Roy growled. "I have..." He tapped the tobacco from his pipe and prepared to mount the gangway of a Norwegian freighter.

Boyle frowned. He couldn't understand Roy's attitude toward his own son. In his opinion, Joe Hawkins was only doing what all of them should do – have a go at authority. Jack was a rebel out and out. Only his hatred for Ed Black saved him from being classified as a militant – plus, of course, his friendship for Roy. He needed somebody like Hawkins to temper his viciousness; his addiction to causing trouble.

An hour later, Jack found himself forced to work with Ed. In a far corner of the hold, Roy slaved with a dedication Jack found sickening.

"Christ, doesn't 'e know when to stop?"

Ed Black welcomed the opportunity to take a break. He wasn't a man who enjoyed hard labour nor did he consider it necessary to kill oneself for the employing body. His creed was simple – "higher pay for less work." Productivity agreements were, to him, a means to an end. They sounded fine on an engineering contract but, in reality, they meant absolute zero in action. His brother in the *Mirror* had kept him informed of *their* productivity agreements and it was a family laugh when they discussed the way that union had buffaloed the government's prices and incomes policy.

"'E's a blackleg, Jack. I don't trust 'im."

Boyle moved away, wishing to hell he hadn't opened the door for another Black tirade. Roy and he may not always agree, see eye-to-eye, but they were mates. Which was more than could be said for Ed Black. Ed was nobody's mate. "I wouldn't annoy Roy unless you want to meet up with his son, Joe."

Ed jabbed a finger into Jack's chest. "That little bastard isn't interested in the likes o' me. 'E ain't even worried about 'is old man."

"It isn't wot Roy said," Jack threw back, hopefully. "I wouldn't annoy Joe Hawkins. Not ever!" He shook his head thoughtfully.

Ed Black was thoughtful too. He was big, strong, had taken care of himself in some weird corners of the globe. As the union representative, he could count on certain heavies to protect him during a strike. His cronies would always rally round his particular flag, too. Yet – the mention of Joe Hawkins sent a shiver of fear down his spine. He couldn't understand this modern generation. Violence was a natural part of life as a docker saw it but the style of brutality these kids employed frightened him silly. Fists and the occasional kick happened; clubs with nails sticking through, and boots specifically meant for inflicting serious injury, were something else again. It wasn't just Joe Hawkins that worried him. One yellow-spined kid would never worry the likes of him. But Joe had a mob and even he was forced to admit that one man was no match for a bunch of savage little bastards ready to tear an individual apart just for fun.

"I'll talk to Roy," Ed said softly, moving away from Boyle.

Jack grinned. Slumping against grain sacks, he waited for Ed to return. When the union specified it took two men to lift what an old-time docker would have considered an easy weight, Jack believed in obeying rules. Two men it would be; and every lost minute meant a fatter pay-packet anyway!

Joe Hawkins hated his parents with all the violence in his young body. Especially, he loathed his father's attitude to life. What, he asked himself as he washed meticulously, had his dad gained from being a soft touch? The house they lived in was far removed from a palace. It was small, cramped, in an awful street. The neighbours were old, foul-mouthed and unintelligent. Not that Joe felt that he possessed a good measure of intelligence. He admitted, but only to himself, that his education had suffered badly. But he was foxy clever. He had a native intelligence that would carry him to heights his father had not inspired to reach. Plaistow and its dirt were not for Joe. One day, he would move away and never return. His sights were set on a plush flat somewhere near the West End. But that required money, and social position. And, as yet, he had neither, although his day was coming. Of that he was positive...

"Joe... you upstairs?"

He turned from his wardrobe mirror and scowled at the partially open door. His mother sounded in a vile temper – as usual!

"Yeah."

"Come down 'ere."

His hand automatically reached inside his shirt for the comforting feel of the tool stuck in his trousers' waistband. He was proud of it. He had taken a week to make the weapon – thick rubber tubing filled with lead-shot and sand, and plugged securely until it was pliable without losing the necessary sting when used. Dropping his shirt over the cosh he slowly descended the narrow stairs.

"I arsked you to fetch me bread this mornin'," his mother snarled. She waved a loaf before his face, "'and over the money... this is stale!"

Joe grinned. "It was all they had."

"The money!" Mrs. Hawkins said again, hand outstretched. Joe didn't frighten her. She was one of those heavy women with massive forearms and a determination to match her girth. She had been born in Plaistow and fought for everything she had.

All her life, Thelma Hawkins had known poverty and hardship. Unlike her husband Roy, Thelma did not have cause to trust her neighbours nor believe in anything except herself. Even her son was an object of suspicion where it came to money.

"I ain't got it," Joe sulked.

Thelma's heavy hand swung, catching the lad across his cheek. "Joe," and she breathed heavily, "I'm not arskin' a second time."

The boy's hand dipped into his pocket and handed over a coin. Thelma sighed, fingered the coin as a priest would a statue of the infant Jesus. "Next time I arsk you..."

"I won't bleedin' go!"

Returning to his room, Joe contemplated his face in the mirror. Her hand-marks showed red. "The old cow" he muttered, fondling his cosh, wishing to hell he could get enough courage to use it on her. Pleasant dreams flooded his mind – and, he saw his hand streaking down, the cosh a blur as it slashed across her cheek, the sound of cracking a satisfactory end to a fleeting wish.

He fingered his face momentarily, then swung from the mirror with an exclamation of frustration.

Opening the wardrobe, he selected his gear from its shadowy recesses...

Union shirt – collarless and identical to thousands of others worn by his kind throughout the country; army trousers and braces; and boots! The boots were the most important item. Without his boots, he was part of the common-herd – like his dad, a working man devoid of identity. Joe was proud of *his* boots. Most of his mates wore new boots bought for a high price in a High Street shop. But not Joe's. His were genuine army-disposal boots; thick-soled, studded, heavy to wear and heavy to feel if slammed against a rib.

It was Saturday and West Ham were playing Chelsea at Stamford Bridge. He wished the match had been at Upton Park. A lot of his mates had stopped travelling across London to Chelsea's ground. Funny, he thought, how the balance of "power" had shifted from East to West in a few years. He remembered when the Krays had been king-pins of violence in London and the East End had ruled the roost. Not now! Every section of the sprawling city had its claim to fame. South of the Thames the niggers rode cock-a-hoop in Brixton; the Irish held Shepherd's Bush with an iron fist; and the Jews predominated around Hampstead and Golders Green. The Cockney had lost control of his London. Even Soho had gone down the drain of provincial invasion. The pimps and touts there weren't old-established Londoner types. They came from Scouseland, Malta, Cyprus and Jamaica. Even the porno shops were having their difficulties with the parasitic influx of outside talent.

Like most of his generation, Joe *knew* about these things. At one time, East Enders enjoyed a visit to Soho and mingling with the "heavy boys" from Poplar and Plaistow and Barking. No longer. The word had circulated – stay away from Soho. Look for your heroes in Ilford, Forest Gate and Whitechapel. The old cockney thug was slowly being confined – to Bow, Mile End, Bethnal Green and their fringe areas. London was wide open now. To anyone with a gun, a cosh, an army of thugs.

Joe was brash enough to venture forth into enemy territory. He had seven mates – all tooled for trouble; all asking the same question: "Any aggro today?"

Slipping a light-weight cotton jacket over his gear, Joe studied himself in the mirror. The cosh didn't show under the jacket. He fingered his West Ham scarf, then threw it back into his wardrobe. *That* would be asking for police inspection... and the last thing he wanted was having his cosh found before he had an opportunity to use it.

He wasn't a bad-looking youth. At sixteen, he gave the impression of being at least nineteen. He was tall for his age – five-eleven. He had filled out and, at a fleeting glance, many a young girl's heart would flutter when he appeared on the scene. But his eyes could have deterred those females wary of sadistic companions. There was something in his gaze that spoke of brutality and nonconformity expressed in terms of physical rejection and explosive reaction.

At last, he was ready. Taking a final glance at his appearance, he nodded to his image, grinning approval. Then, with heavy boots making a resounding noise on the worn stair-carpet, he went to the front door, yelled: "I'm goin'," And left.

Outside, on the street, he paused.

God, how he hated this street! Next door, he could see that bitch Grace peeping from behind her curtains. What a bloody bitch she was! No matter how he acted, nor what he thought, he hated her for the way she had treated her husband. In a way, though, he was afraid of Grace. In his opinion, she was a black witch – and he didn't want to associate with her!

He hurried down the street, conscious of eyes following him. It was always the same. No matter how early he left the house, eyes always followed him. Sometimes he wondered if they ever slept in his dirty street.

He was whistling when he strolled down to the Barking Road. The cosh felt comfortable against his flesh. His boots felt solid, secure on his feet. In a few minutes he would meet his mates and, soon, they would be ready for aggro...

# CHAPTER TWO

FRESH AIR in the pub was more valuable than gold dust. Smoke from countless pipes and smouldering cigarettes filled both bars, effectively helping to dull the clinging smell of cheap disinfectant. Nobody had ever asked the guvnor to list his establishment as a must on a tourist itinerary. It was unlikely anyone ever would.

If air was precious, a sentence spoken without four-letter emphasis was enough to bring sudden silence, raised eyebrows and get the speaker an award for bravery in the face of obscenity. Even the two barmaids spoke in anatomical descriptiveness and some of their suggestions were physical impossibilities except for a mechanical engineer.

His mates had the Saturday corner table and Joe shoved through the crowd, catching sight of Henry Downy at the bar. "Pint, mate," he yelled, getting a nod from the pimpled youth. Frankly, he couldn't stand the sight of Henry. The guy's pimples wanted to make him throw-up. Not just that, though – he had serious doubts about Henry's usefulness to the mob. He had always kept a close eye on Henry's activities and never ever gave advance information of an aggro when Henry was listening.

"You tooled?" Billy Endine asked nervously as he took his chair.

"Of course," Joe replied with an indignant sneer. "Think I'd go to fuckin' Chelsea without this?" His hand fondled the cosh under his shirt.

Billy shrugged and watched Henry struggle through the crowd with their beer. None of the boys tried to help the pimpled youth. It wasn't part of being mates to offer a helping hand. Not in their mob, anyway. "'Enery ain't got 'is!"

Joe fixed Henry with a malicious eye. He watched how the beer slopped on the table as the other nervously set it before him. "Wot's this about you not 'aving a tool?"

Henry glanced over his shoulder then spoke in a whisper. "My old man found it. Jeeze, didn't 'e raise hell!"

"You're a bleedin' liar, mate," Joe said deliberately. "Go get a tool or forget the game." His hand closed possessively round the glass, his mocking smile destroying Henry's unspoken reply in advance. As the pimple-face youth walked dejectedly away, Joe laughed. "Serves the bastard right! Drink up lads… 'is beer is good!"

From behind the bar, Mary Sommers watched the group. She couldn't take her gaze off Billy and, she felt sure, he was returning her interest each time he glanced across the pub. She was nearly old enough to be his mother but it didn't stop her having physical yearnings for him. It hadn't made her say no two weeks previously when Billy accosted her after closing. Nor had she tried to get away when he seemed to tire of feeling her. In fact, she could admit to herself that it was her prompting that had seen their confrontation develop into a frantic mating behind the soaring Point flats.

She knew she was asking for trouble getting involved with one of them yet her knees shook when she thought about how wonderful it had been pressed against his hard young body. Looking at Joe and the others she even wished Billy would waylay her tonight and share her with his mates. The escapade with Billy had opened floodgates inside her; made her realise how tame the past ten years had been with a man who really never gave sex a thought. She could remember when she was eighteen. Her proud boast then had been "I've been screwed by every man in the district". Since her marriage, she'd had about six bits on the side – hardly enough for a healthy, passionate woman with her shape.

Bending to pour a pint, she became aware of eyes peering down her wide-fronted blouse. She looked up, and caught the old lecher leaning forward to see more of her breasts. He turned away, smiling secretly. He'd had his eyeful and that was his fair share. At seventy-three a man could look but not touch.

Mary shrugged, her breasts jiggling firmly. The motion did not go un-noted. Those closest to the bar grinned; those at tables tried to catch her act but she refused to co-operate, her attention still rivetted on Billy and his mates.

"You don't want little bastards like them, Mary-girl!"

She swung on the man. "Mind your own fuckin' business," she snapped.

The man frowned. "Christ, lads – she's really after Joe!"

Let them get it wrong, Mary thought, flouncing down the bar. They'll be trying to catch me with Roy's son and I'll be rubbing against Billy. *God*, she sighed. *I wish I was!*

"That old cow!" Billy snorted disgustedly. "I jumped her an' she raped *me*."

Joe twisted round, studying Mary with a lascivious eye. He had to admit she looked pretty good for a tart. Turning to Billy he grinned. "Was it good?"

"I've had worse."

"Arrange to meet her and we'll all be there..."

Billy frowned. "If she hollers, Joe..."

"Bloody hell, she's only a wet-knickered bitch! She won't holler. Go ahead – talk to her."

Billy got to his feet looking dubious. It was one thing trying to get a bit in the dark for yourself, he thought, but letting Joe and his other mates share – well, that was asking for big trouble. Since hanging had been abolished some magistrates were getting bleeding horrible with the amount of porridge they handed out. Especially when it involved tear-aways and girls! Bloody M.P.s, he thought. They got elected to do what their constituents wanted done and the bastards thought they were little tin-gods better than the voters! If he had his way every politician would be slung into prison and given a taste of what they deserved.

"Hey, Mary..." He leant against the bar between two huge coloured men. The stink of the blacks made him sick. He hated spades – wished they'd wash more often or get the hell back where they came from. This was *his* London – not somewhere for London Transport's African troops to live. He enjoyed the occasional aggro in Brixton. Smashing a few wog heads open always gave him greater satisfaction than bashing those bleeding Chelsea supporters.

Mary slopped beer into a glass and pushed it at her customer. She felt her knees go rubbery. Collecting the cash, she rang it up, then hurried along the bar to face Billy. Her eyes sparkled, her breasts heaved.

"Same again for the lads," Billy muttered, unable to tear his gaze from those beauties. It wasn't his round yet he couldn't come right out with the proposition. Joe's insistence on making Mary made him think about the other night and he suddenly realised how good it had been. Why should he share her with his mates?

"Billy wants to see you again, Mary..."

Billy glowered at Joe standing beside him now. Mary didn't flinch. She stared at Joe, asked softly, "Will you be there too?"

Joe nodded.

"When, Billy?"

The boy was lost. He couldn't understand a woman like her. He'd had his share of the little bits hanging around the fringes of their mob – the local girls trying to snare one of the better-known heroes. He'd even gone to bed with a Soho brass when they'd pulled a job off. But that had been a big disappointment. He'd felt sick, feeling around a professional tart.

"Tonight... when you finish here?" Joe asked.

Mary felt her throat constrict. She glanced up and down the bar. "Wait for me behind the Point?"

"We'll be there – won't we, Billy?"

Billy wanted to object. Knowing Joe, the woman would be subjected to extremes of intercourse before he – or any of the others – got their share. Yet, nobody denied Joe Hawkins his glory. "Yeah, Joe, that's fine."

Mary lowered her voice. "Forget this round – it's on me."

Joe laughed, returning to his seat. Mary would fiddle it. They were getting free beer on the guvnor for promising to give her what all concerned would thoroughly enjoy – especially Mary. The round was on her and everything else pleasurable would be on her, too.

The coloured man beside Billy laughed throatily, slapped Billy's shoulder. "Man, you'se got it made," he grinned.

Billy brushed the hand away and glared at the man. "Don't ever touch me, spade!" He backed away, ready to grab his tool.

Quickly, the two coloured men stiffened and moved to close in on their opponent. Then, suddenly – as the pub grew deathly silent – they glanced around and relaxed with foolish grins on their ebony faces. Even they had heard about Joe Hawkins, and his mob.

"Trouble, Billy?" Joe asked eagerly, watching the coloured men with what amounted to hungry appreciation. Like most East End skinheads – and, for that matter, population – Joe detested the influx of immigrants into what had always been a pure Cockney stronghold. It wasn't so much the colour of the skins that annoyed him. Any intruder would have been subject to the same treatment – be the man South African, Canadian, American. The East End was proud of its London-heritage; afraid to lose its ancient right to control what was, essentially, a Saxon bastion. 'Anglo-' had never been acceptable here. Loyalty to an established, accredited Cockney crown was taken for granted. In time of war, the East Ender had only to enter a recruiting office to be accepted as a fit example of a British fighting man. Nobody dare question that. Nor the right an East Ender had to voice his opinion regardless of Race Relations Board and governmental sympathies. Spades or wogs didn't count. They were impositions on the face of a London that should always be white, Cockney, true-British... not so-called British because they claimed a passport and insisted on rights their independent nations did not grant to the inhabitants of the British Isles.

"No trouble, man," the first immigrant said.

"None," his fellow black murmured.

Joe grinned evilly. He wasn't satisfied to let it go at that. This was Saturday – a day for splitting skulls. What better warm-up than these two coons...

"Apologize..." he suggested antagonistically, moving forward with his mob stepping in tight like a gang of Nazi S.S. men about to interrogate a prisoner.

Billy grinned. He felt tall, more than equal to a couple of hefty niggers now he had the backing of Joe and the lads. "Tell me how sorry you fuckin' well are," he snarled.

The first negro blanched. He lived in Plaistow and knew how difficult it could be to oppose this gang of young thugs. He had heard of other immigrants whose homes had been terrorized. He had been warned by the pastor not to invite racial discontent with the 'ignorant' Londoner. Mentally, he rejected these white savages – and all Englishmen – as inferiors striving to prove their right to subjugate black peoples. He didn't stop to think about the poverty and superstition that made his homeland a place to avoid, or leave, nor the debt each of his people owed to the British administrators, the British tax-payer, the British sense of fair-play. He forgot these things because he wanted a job, a decent home – even if, after occupation, he turned it into a slum-dwelling – and a right to stand on his own feet without having a witch-doctor, a tribal chieftain, or an arrogant headman telling him what to do, when to do it, how to do it. He remembered his rights in England – the right to protest and call the British bastards and exploiters.

"I'se sorry, *boss*," he snarled.

Joe laughed. "Boss? Sambo – get stuffed!" He turned away in disgust. The Chelsea mob would offer more resistance.

Billy puffed out his skinny chest and pushed past the coloured men.

Conversation started again in the pub and Mary's eyes glittered frantically as she kept watching Joe, Billy and the mob. These were her type of men, she thought. She loathed serving blacks. She detested their lecherous looks, their arrogant attempts to strip her across the bar and the almost "don't dare refuse me" propositions they made. But the guvnor had warned her not to invite trouble by refusing to serve them.

# CHAPTER THREE

WAITING FOR the District Line train to come in, Joe regarded his mob with a critical gaze. They were not an inseparable group. Billy and Don usually accompanied him on big bovver but Tony, Jack, Frank and Harry usually managed to avoid the more audacious escapades and shrank from physical contact with opposing forces of numerical superiority. As the leader, Joe felt his mob needed some backbone. It was disastrous to turn for support and find no-one there.

"We gave those spades something to think about, eh, Joe?" Billy laughed as they gathered outside the waiting room.

Joe shrugged. He wasn't interested in the niggers now. They were past tense; his mind was on present and future trouble. "Forget the bastards, Billy," he cautioned. His mind searched for something to vent his spite upon. His gaze lit upon the station sign: UPTON PARK. He grinned. That's what they needed – a sign to tease those Stamford Bridge yobs. "Tony, Jack, nick that sign!" he commanded.

Grinning, the two hurried off, tearing the metal sign from its moorings.

From his relatively safe position on the opposite platform, a stationman took a quick step forward, then slunk back to his post with studious concern for counting the small change people offered in lieu of correct fare. Six weeks previously he had been brave and tried to defeat the vandalism of these young thugs. Not any more. London Transport didn't pay him enough to wage single-handed war against savages. Nor did he consider contacting the police any solution, either. He didn't want them waiting for him after a night-shift. Occasionally, he glanced furtively across the track to see what they were up to next. He would have to make a report but that was going to be the extent of his involvement in the affair.

He would never know what his lack of involvement was going to cost his employer – nor the agony to one of his fellow-workers!

"WEST HAM... WEST HAM... WEST HAM..." The mob chanted as they poured into a carriage when the train arrived.

Other supporters laughed, took separate carriages – content in the thought that they were better off not riding with Joe Hawkins. Yet, they didn't find the mob's actions contrary to accepted behaviour for football supporters. None of them belonged to an official body attached to their club. That would be tantamount to accepting authority and civilized conduct – and these were anathema for the likes of Joe and other young tearaways.

Joe glared at the occupants of his carriage. Native cunning warned him that L.T. sometimes planted one of their trains likely to carry football supporters. He didn't give a damn about one man but he didn't wish to be trapped below ground when the dogs came. Boots and a tool meant nothing to a ferocious dog but flashing teeth meant a whole lot of pain for a skinhead.

Like frozen puppets, the other passengers sat in their seats, trying hard to forget Joe's presence. The fat woman with shopping bags glared right back at him then, conscious of the strained atmosphere as the train started, dropped her gaze and concentrated on the tips of her shoes. A small man wearing a scarf and hat examined the route map, reading and re-reading the names of stations listed. A young mother with two children suddenly discovered wonders outside the window to bring to their attention. A tall, portly gentleman in a window seat refused to be intimidated and stared at the mob until Joe's slow grin changed his mind. A newspaper opened and the man's face got lost in the spreading printed pages.

A man and woman sitting almost directly opposite Joe continued to discuss matters of intimate importance until Joe leered at the woman. She was tall, blonde, beautiful, and showed a neat pair of pins. She flushed and turned her head. The man, who was slightly shorter than his wife and looked as if he could take care of himself in a fight, turned and glowered at Joe. In a loud voice he asked his wife, "Is this layabout bothering you, hon?"

The woman muttered something too low for Joe to hear but he didn't give a damn. He had his target – the man. He didn't like people calling him a layabout nor did he like men to think they could put him in his place.

"Hey, Don – what about this piece?"

Don Taylor broke off his discussion about Bobby Moore's merits and stared at the woman. He smiled and gestured obscenely. "A bleedin' shame she's got 'im!"

"Shit on 'im!" Joe retorted. "She fancies you mate..."

Don moved down the carriage until he stood leaning on the seat the couple occupied. "That true, missus?"

The man got to his feet. There was no hurry in his movements and this lulled Don into false security. Anyway what did he have to fear? He had his mates...

"You bloody little swine," The man snarled and, without warning, his fist whipped upwards in a perfect uppercut to land under Don's jutting chin. Like a sack of grain, Don folded, slammed back across the carriage, and collapsed into Joe's lap. The train swayed, then slowed for the next station.

The woman gasped, hand reaching to touch her husband's sleeve but he shook it off angrily. "All right, you bastards!" he snarled. "Let's see how brave you are..."

Joe dumped the floundering Don on the floor, got to his feet, hand coming from inside his shirt with the deadly tool ready for its vicious work. Like clockwork soldiers, his mob filtered down the carriage, forming a semi-circle round the lone passenger. "You arsked for this, mister," Joe growled, whipping his tool against one palm, feeling the satisfying smack of it on flesh. "Pile in, lads..."

The man fought like a tiger. He caught several blows on extended forearms, landed his own counter-punches with devastating results but he was outnumbered and, slowly, he was forced back... back... almost into his wife's lap. Her screams didn't help him. Her struggles to avoid battering blows hindered him.

Joe grinned, feeling his cosh bounce off the man's temple, seeing blood spurt.

Frank landed a boot into the man's thigh hearing the agonized gasp.

The fat woman yelled, and leapt up to pull the communication cord.

The tall, portly man flung his newspaper aside, got to his feet, saw blood pouring from the man's face and slumped back into his seat – ashamed of himself but safe in the knowledge it wasn't his personal fight.

The man fought to get away from his hysterical wife... head down, charging into the slashing, kicking, maddened mob of attackers.

The train jerked to a halt, the doors sliding open.

The fat woman exploded onto the platform, screaming for help – her exit not adding to the excitement *inside* the carriage as the mob battered their enemy with relentless fury.

Running to the fat woman, a coloured guard felt himself pulled unwittingly to the scene of carnage. He had been warned by his union not to tackle rampaging fans on his own – but to call for police reinforcements and take a back seat regardless of what happened. Unfortunately, the fat woman decided otherwise and shoved him into the carriage, screaming for "somebody to do something to save that courageous man from those vicious thugs in there".

Joe saw the guard and stepped back. As though telepathically controlled, his mates retreated from the man, leaving him clawing for support as he folded over a seat, face streaming blood, body battered and bruised where heavy boots had taken their toll.

"A coon! A fuckin' coon!" Joe hissed, edging forward, suspicious yet sure the police had not been called this soon.

"Wha's wrong here?" the guard asked timorously.

Joe laughed, jabbing the guard's chest with a stiff finger, his cosh held in readiness down one thigh. "Beat it, coon! This ain't your business!"

The beaten man's wife stood huddled against a window, her face expressing the revulsion and fear welling inside her. She pointed, yelled: "Arrest them... can't you see what they've done to Jim?"

The guard felt a hard lump fill his throat. He could see what had happened – and he didn't want the same treatment for himself.

"Wot you goin' to do, mate?" Joe asked deliberately.

The guard swallowed. "Off the train, son..."

Joe's cosh lashed out, striking the hapless guard across the cheek. The crunch of breaking bone was a glorious sound for Joe's mob. Like a pack of wolves they swarmed forward, bent on the kill. Boots found their target, tools slashed viciously, fists landed with dull, sickening thuds. The guard wasn't a fighter. Not like the woman's husband. He melted away as the mob pushed forward, trampling him under foot.

"Leave the coon bastard," Joe yelled, surging through the open doors. "Let's get a bus!" He raced down the platform, scattering those passengers who had dared view the incident.

Billy – always one to take advantage of a beaten man – aimed a kick at the guard's groin, felt his boot sink in with devastating impact. He grinned, got ready to land a second blow... and then screamed as a hard fist slammed against his eye. Pain lanced through him and he stumbled from the carriage, yelling for his mates...

"Darling... oh, darling... don't!"

The woman grabbed her husband, clung to him, preventing him from following the fleeing mob. From the floor, the guard tried to gauge the situation, struggled to his feet and was immediately sick all over the place. His groin hurt terribly.

From the sanctuary of his newspaper, the tall portly man muttered: "It's about time the law did something to curb this violence. Young thugs... should be taught a lesson!" He didn't even glance down at the stricken guard nor the bloody face of the husband, still determined to protect his wife and fight on against impossible odds. He didn't realise it, but the tall, portly man was a statistic – just one of those who had allowed the likes of Joe Hawkins to rise to fame; one of the masses unwilling to share responsibility for putting teenage hoodlums in their place and safe-guarding the nation from a wave of anti-social brutality. In a time of war, the man would have risen to meet the challenge yet he was unable to see that this conflict between the young and the State was, in fact, all-out war. A war threatening the authority that a country needed to keep it stable.

*

"Did you see how I booted 'im?" Billy asked.

"Yeah, mate," Don answered, eager for praise for his own efforts. "You saw me bust 'is head, didn'tcha?"

"You was terrific," Jack enthused. He glanced at Joe, anxious to please their leader. "Mate," he slapped Joe's back, "you got 'im good. God, 'ow he bleedin' well yelled when you caught him!"

Joe felt proud. His home-made tool had come through with honours. Blood flecked its length – that bastard's blood! He didn't enjoy thinking about how the man had withstood all their battering and still kept fighting back. He didn't like knowing that some men had more guts inside them than what his mob had in total.

Billy felt his eye. It would be black tomorrow. It hurt. "Fuckin' bastard!" he growled to himself. "I'd like to go back an' do 'im." He wasn't proud of himself when he touched the eye. He didn't pretend to be tough, nor brave, nor able to handle himself right inside where he lived. For show, though, he acted like he was Henry Cooper – fit fighting man, ready to take on all comers. Especially, he acted hard when with Joe. That Joe, he thought – nothing scares him!


"What can we do, sir?" the policeman asked the bleeding man. "We don't know who they are…"

James Mowat dabbed at the blood trickling down his cheek, and felt the pain increase as his wife tried to stem the flow, too. "Isn't it about time you banned football supporters from using the Underground?"

"Ah, that would be difficult, sir," the constable replied. "Who can tell who is a supporter and who is a skinhead…"

"Skinhead?" Mowat asked.

"The ones who attacked you, sir," said the patient constable, "were skinheads. You've described how they were dressed. That's skinhead gear, sir."

Mowat shrugged. "I don't give a damn what you call them – why should innocent people be forced to share the same carriage with animals like that?"

"It's a problem of our times, sir…"

"The hell it is!" The man erupted.

Constable Monteeth was young, capable, dedicated. If he had been otherwise he would not be wearing his uniform. He readily sympathised with the battered man but he didn't believe in countering violence with more violence. He believed, as his superiors had taught him to believe, in the British policeman's duty to temper violence with understanding – and therein lay his problem. He could not reason that consideration for these thugs gave them a feeling of confidence, that it added to their determination to make fools of the law, society and their fellow men. He could not see that the teenage hoodlums needed strict measures and stricter punishment when caught in the act. He believed injustice without going further to see how the other side looked on justice as a blind, foppish old nanny administering a gentle slap when a cane should be used. He paid heed to the do-gooders who would treat all problems as the result of traumatic experiences in childhood and who would ban hanging for the most heinous crimes and institute psychotherapy instead of the birch.

"Yes, sir," The constable remarked with a lack of feeling. "Now, if you could come to the station..."

"To hell with that!" Mowat exclaimed. "What good will it do? You'll not lift a finger to apprehend the thugs and, even supposing you catch 'em – what'll they get? Ten pounds fine and the Social Security pays it from my taxes? Hell, man – can't you see what this bloody Welfare State is costing Britain?"

Joe stuck his feet on the front of the bus. From here he would be able to watch London jerking past; see the sights tourists paid a fortune to come see. None of the monuments nor architectural beauties made any impression on Joe. He was ignorant of historical heritage, believing in modern sterile sky-scrapers as the ultimate in construction. The Bank of England only reached him as a source of ill-gotten loot; St. Paul's as a symbol of London and not a church dedicated to the advancement of Godliness within his City; Nelson's Column as a roosting place for dropping-birds and not the heroic valour that had made his homeland great; Admiralty Arch as a traffic hold-up and not the remaining splendour of a navy that had once ruled the waves. Joe, like his teenage hoodlums, had forgotten the greatness and the adventure that had given him and his ancestors that sense of pride which came from expansion, world domination, democratic rule.

For the most part, Joe and his mob loudly speculated about the sexual attributes of mini-skirted girls walking along The Strand, through Trafalgar Square, down Whitehall. When they were not doing this they concentrated on causing a disturbance with the other passengers on the top-deck – especially to the annoyance of a small, Dresden-doll girl with a perfect figure and a nice pair of thighs.

"Cor, doll," Joe drooled, arm over the back of his seat, eyes feasting on the girl's limbs, "won'tcha meet me tonight?" He leered where – just faintly – her panties could be seen. "I could make it luverly for you!"

The girl blushed, turned her head and tried to find interest in the Houses of Parliament.

A military-type wearing an officer's coat grunted to the conductor and remarked, "I say, isn't it time you gave those young thugs a warning to behave?"

The conductor glanced at the first three seats, carefully avoiding a direct confrontation. "They're just high-spirited..." he mumbled, wishing that some people would mind their own bloody business.

"They haven't paid their fares," a stout woman snapped.

The conductor blanched. He *knew* that. He'd asked several times "any more fares" and they had done nothing to give him the idea that they intended paying. Normally, he didn't take any nonsense from layabouts and yobbos but he had been on the Brixton run two weeks previously and got a nasty punch for daring to request fares. Now, he knew better than to antagonize thugs. "They have, missus," he said, hurrying down the bus.

"Not so bleedin' fast," the stout woman shouted, grabbing the conductor's arm. "Make 'em show their tickets. Why should the likes of us pay if they don't?"

The conductor's jaw muscles tightened. He had prayed this moment wouldn't come...

"Fares, please," he said advancing on the mob.

Not one of them even glanced in his direction.

"Excuse me, sir..." The conductor murmured, standing over Frank Cooper.

"Fuck off," The boy snarled.

The conductor bristled. The beating was forgotten. He didn't like yobbos to start with and he didn't enjoy being spoken to in this manner in front of his passengers. "Tickets, please..." he snapped, instantly sorry as Frank turned around and laughed up at him.

Joe got from his seat, stood in the aisle facing the flustered conductor. "Wot's wrong?" he asked belligerently.

"Nothing – if you've got tickets," the other replied.

"We ain't – so wot?"

The conductor wanted to turn, run down the stairs and consult with his driver. He couldn't. The passengers behind him were glaring, waiting for him to assert his authority; consciously willing him to toss these young tearaways off the bus. "Where did you get on?"

Joe sneered. "Last stop, mate."

"That's a lie," The stout woman yelled.

Joe glared at the woman. It was his day for bumping into fat, old cows determined to cause trouble for him. "Fuck you, missus!" he shouted back.

The military-type got to his feet. "I say..." he began.

"Fares, please," the conductor interrupted, hands ready to issue tickets from his machine.

Joe shoved the man aside, shouted, "Our stop," And started walking down the aisle. Like automatons, the gang rose, followed their leader, each one making sure he pushed against the conductor, each pausing by the stout woman to laugh.

"Christ, Joe – we didn't have to get orf," Jack Holly complained as they stood watching the bus grow smaller in the distance.

"Look, mate," Joe replied firmly. "We want to see the match, don't we?"

Jack nodded.

"Then we don't want trouble with the fuzz until we get to Stamford Bridge, do we?"

Jack smiled. "Gee, Joe – you think of everything!"

*

Joe did think of everything. A bunch of skinheads entering the ground together would certainly attract the notice of coppers near the turnstiles. The group split – into pairs, Joe taking Billy Endine with him. Without West Ham scarves, acting innocent as new-born babes and trying to affect a nonchalance the police would overlook, Joe and Billy managed to slip past the scrutinizing eyes of the fuzz.

Don and Jack were unlucky. They got turned away, screaming protests, accusing the fuzz of being petty dictators and arousing the Chelsea fans to such a pitch that they got turned over before taking their hasty departure.

Tony and Frank, playing it safe, got in and joined with their mates.

Now they were four – all bent on mayhem; each wanting to vent his spite on the nearest Chelsea supporter.

"I don't like this place," Frank muttered, gazing around him.

Joe had reached the same conclusion but now that Frank had voiced his opinion it was imperative he – as their leader – should decide. "It's okay," he grumbled, casting nervous glances at the fanatic Chelsea fans gathered about them. He could tell the others were equally bent on trouble – the standardized uniforms, the close-cropped heads, the boots, all spoke of opposition skinheads.

If Joe had but known!

For miles around the ground the word SHED was emblazoned on gables, walls, poster sites. It meant something in this area – a warning for those wishing to watch a match in quiet contemplation to stay clear of that area of Stamford Bridge commonly called The Shed. It was here that the fanatic supporters gathered, in their gear and with boots ready to inflict injury on opposing factions.

And it was there that Joe and his mates gathered! Unaware of the consequences they faced if, just once, they let their West Ham feelings erupt...

The man was alone, loud-mouthed and eager for crowd support when he glorified Chelsea's record in the league. He didn't mean to be offensive; he was an ordinary fan squeezed in with a bunch of savages. He tried to get crowd-sympathy for his tolerant club support – not honestly wishing more than a clean, well-fought game. He wanted his neighbours to yell for victory but was willing to go home relatively content if the match should end with Chelsea a goal down. Always providing, of course, the game was clean, hard-fought, played in the spirit of football.

In The Shed he was asking for a miracle if he wanted his support to be fair-minded and free from trouble!

Unaware that the boys behind him were avid West Ham supporters and boiling for a fight, he turned to Joe, grinned, and asked, "Ain't they the best?"

Joe laughed. His fingers closed round his tool, and eased it from under his union-shirt. "Yeah," he muttered, pointing with his free hand to the pitch. "There they come..."

The fan turned, and as he did, Joe whipped the cosh from his shirt and cracked it across the man's ear. He saw blood spurt – felt greatness descend upon him. *First blood to West Ham!*

The fan slumped.

Tony leered, slamming his boot squarely into the man's backside as he fell.

Billy – not to be outdone – kicked viciously, catching the man in the chest. His next blow broke the man's jaw – the crunch bringing a measure of satisfaction.

Like quicksilver, the message whipped around The Shed: "Tool up – the enemy's here!"

The kid next to Joe was no more than thirteen, and small. He had a close-cropped haircut and new boots. He had a sharp hunk of steel in his right hand, knuckledusters on his left hand. As the man slumped and fell under scuffling feet, the kid lunged at Joe, the sharpened steel finding its target in the ribs, the knucks flashing as they headed for Joe's chin. Joe ducked, pain lancing through his side. His cosh curved across the kid's tender cheek, smashing bone. Then it slammed down, busting the skull. Blood trickled down Joe's side, making him groggy.

"That's another of the fuckin' bastards!" screamed a Chelsea fan. His boot landed on Billy's hip, his tool finding the enemy's shoulder – the nails digging in with agonizing force.

Billy buckled, clawing at his shoulder. He could feel the rusted nails biting deep, screwed as the Chelsea skinhead tried to withdraw his weapon for another attack.

Billy screamed. He wanted to vomit as a boot landed right in his balls.

Joe yelled as a bottle exploded in his face – a jagged-broken bottle pushed at him with savage force. He felt his skin yield, crack, blood spurt. His cosh flicked... swung in a blind circle as the Chelsea fans swarmed in on him.

Tony and Frank battled gamely – clearing a path for the *hors de combat* duo struggling in their wake.

At the turnstile, Joe wavered. He didn't enjoy being victimized, nor sent packing without getting in a few licks of his own. The cosh in his hand itched to crack a few more skulls – yet the blood pouring down his face needed attention.

"Come on, mate," Frank coaxed. "Let's have a beer, eh?"

Joe accepted the out, pushed through the turnstile and hurried past an observant copper. The first cheers for the teams sounded from the ground.

"We won anyway, Joe," Billy grinned.

Joe glared at his companion, ready to argue the point but unwilling to make an issue right then. Once he stopped the flow of blood he would be in a better position to stress that opinion. He nodded, holding his handkerchief to his slashed face. "Yeah," he mouthed. "Yeah – we won!"

# CHAPTER FOUR

THEY'D HAD AN eventful journey back on the Underground. Fortunately, they were earlier than the police estimated trouble would begin. They'd terrorized a few passengers, slashed a dozen or so seats and broken the normal number of windows before reaching East Ham. There, they alighted and scared the hell out of the ticket-collector by stealing his small change from those who preferred to pay short instead of purchasing tickets at their boarding station.

Once outside the station, Joe decided to visit a bookie. He had heard one of his mates talking about a certain horse and he figured a few quid on it wouldn't go astray.

The bookie's office wasn't far from the station and it was packed. Joe scribbled his bet, handed it across the counter to a cute blonde and tried to date her for the night. When she refused he got mad – threatening to tear the place apart until a thick-set gent in loud tweed stepped forward and told him to "Get lost, sonny". He got lost – and when Frank returned with the news that his horse had lost by fifteen lengths he felt like a dictator who had been ousted from his seat of supreme power.

His one compensation was Mary, the barmaid. Everybody loved Saturday night, he reasoned – especially an old bag wanting a young lover.

"There wasn't much aggro, was there, Joe?" Billy remarked as they wandered down the High Street in search of adventure.

Joe touched his battered face. It had been enough for him. An inch closer and he could have been blind. His cheek hurt, his handkerchief in his pocket felt sodden with blood. His cosh had taken its deadly toll but he'd thirsted for more... much more than The Shed crowd had permitted. God how he hated those Chelsea bastards! If only he had a better mob to support his ambitions! Billy wasn't bad and Frank could use the boot if he got the upper-hand. Tony wasn't eager and Don wanted the odds always in his favour before resorting to violence. Jack and Henry were, in Joe's opinion, non-starters – they screamed before the first blow caught 'em.

"Not bad, mate," Joe said thoughtfully. "Did you see 'ow I got the cunt?"

Billy nodded enthusiastically, saying fast, "You got 'im, Joe. An' I didn't waste time puttin' the boot in, either... eh?"

Joe played the game – the Big Con. "You was terrific, Billy. We was both fantastic..."

"Yeah, Joe – fantastic!"

They searched the shops for signs of easy pickings and found none. The crowds were thick, the shops jammed with Saturday bargain-hunters. In East Ham it didn't pay to look for trouble where people gathered in bunches.

"Wot's the time?"

Billy looked at his watch. "Quarter past five, Joe."

"'Ow about Mary?"

Billy grinned. "She's easy, Joe."

"So?"

Frank rubbed his trousers and yelped, "I'm for her, mate. God, she gives me a hard on!"

Joe grinned. "See, Billy?"

Billy shrugged. He didn't give a damn either way. If Joe wanted Mary he got what was left. If he tried the old cow himself he got nothing that wasn't there after Joe finished. "Yeah... okay!"

"When's she start?" Joe asked.

Billy looked puzzled. "I dunno..."

"Shit! We'll go in soon's they open." Joe stalked down the street, reaching Barking Road. He paused, eyed the traffic coming from London, and wondered if – perhaps – some of the cars had been parked outside Stamford Bridge. He hated the bastards if they had seen the whole match; loathed those Chelsea cunts for getting them involved before the match started.

As he walked, Joe thought. He wasn't completely satisfied with his mob. For one thing, they weren't strong enough. He wanted command of a larger force. Say about forty guys all tooled up and ready to follow where he led. The other mobs had larger forces – he could name dozens like the Willesden Whites, the Hendon Mafia, the Kilburn Aggro Boys. Even in West Ham they had mobs numbering close on fifty qualified bovver boys. He knew what was wrong, though – he needed a helluva bigger reputation before he could see a drift away from established gangs into his own. He had a name but it was too local, too limited. He hadn't done porridge and he hadn't been written up in the papers as an outstanding example of skinhead terrorism. He'd have to do something drastic to make the grade. One big aggro with a reporter present and he'd have them all clamouring to get into his mob.

A Pakistani student approached with an armful of library books under one crooked arm.

Joe grinned, whispering, "Crowd the bastard!"

With undisciplined compliance, his team formed a spearhead smashing through the scattered shoppers. Ten feet away, the Pakistani became aware of the advancing enemy, and hesitated. He didn't have to be reminded of the last exploit involving one of his fellow-students and a skinhead mob – it had made headline news in the Barking paper.

"Ain't he pretty..." Joe laughed.

A small man wearing a scarf and hurrying for his favourite pub abruptly veered into a side-street and took a detour that would not help his thirst for bitter.

A mother with laden shopping bags grabbed her two snotty-nosed kids and ventured across the road regardless of oncoming traffic.

A burly Irishman smiled inwardly, skirted Joe's mob and offered a silent prayer as he stared at the Pakistani and continued on his journey to the boozer.

"Lemme take your books," Joe said, knocking the volumes from the student's arm.

For an instant, the dark face angered then, abruptly, broke into a nervous smile. "Sorry..." he muttered, bending to retrieve his books.

"Bloody wog!" Joe snapped, kicking the Pakistani in the face, knocking him backwards across the pavement. His voice carried above the traffic growl to those watching the all too familiar scene.

"You bleedin' wogs... you don't want us to..." A passing lorry swallowed his words and spat them out in a defiant roar of exhausts.

The Pakistani cowered against a shop window, watchfully aware that the books were being kicked into the road; seeing them flattened under merciless tyres.

"Look wot you done," Joe shouted, grabbing the frightened student. "That costs us money, mate... we pays for your books!" His right caught the Pakistani under the Adam's Apple, his left foot finding the soft underbelly of the other in a vicious kick. "You don't deserve to be 'ere..." He screamed, building to a fever pitch as his feet lashed out with frightening regularity... each blow finding its target.

Like ants swarming over a tasty morsel, the mob crowded the already beaten student, putting the boot in, helping Joe pulverize the Asian. All the hatreds for the newcomers blurred their ability to consider the battered man as a human being – not that they ever considered any target as anything other than a kicking bag for their perverted pleasures.

When it was over – less than three minutes from start to finish – Joe, tired of his kicks, walked away from the stricken Pakistani to get lost in a gathering crowd. One by one, his mob filtered from the scene... vicious shadows flitting into the darkness of evil minds.

The pub was, as usual, jam-packed with Saturday night spenders. Joe felt inferior in the mass of hefty dockers and other assorted heavies. He was smart enough not to force his hand in the middle of such a gathering; he had discovered early in life that a stripling did not gain feathers fighting old cock-birds. These were men accustomed to fisti-cuffs, to putting the boot in, to brawling against odds. They didn't back down to anyone – not even with Joe Hawkins' reputation. Joe could heave sacks of coal around but the weight he could lift was nothing compared to what the average docker thought infantile...

"Your turn, mate," Joe growled to Billy, shoving his empty glass across the table.

Billy got to his feet, feeling for spare change in his pocket.

"An' don't forget to chat-up the old cow," Joe admonished.

Billy fought his way to the bar. He didn't relish the thought of getting Mary outside. He'd had too many beers and all he wanted to do was sleep it off. Beer and sex didn't mix with him – certainly not in the quantities he'd drunk that night. Frankly, he regretted ever mentioning his escapade with Mary. The more alcoholic thought he gave to Mary the more he was convinced that she was a bloody good stand-by when he felt in the mood for cunt. He hat-ed the idea of Joe shoving it into her and him getting seconds. After all, hadn't he been the one who discovered her liking for shafting?

"Billy…"

He leant against the bar with a drunken who-cares stance, affecting those movies with Sinatra playing the short-statured he-man-I-can-handle-'em-all attitude. His bleary eyes beamed on the woman, leering his sexual inclinations like a light-ship warning off ships in the night that pass danger-ously close to perilous sands. "Same again," he said.

"Will you be there?" she asked.

He straightened, and tried standing without the bar to support him. "Of course…"

"Don't drink any more, Billy," she said softly. "I wouldn't want it without you!" She gave him the all-promising eye.

"Joe's first," he said sternly.

"So?"

"He likes it different…"

"So do I, Billy. Won't you do it how *you* like it?"

He sobered fast. "You're big, Mary…"

"I'm smaller other places…" she countered neatly.

Billy wanted to scream. Suddenly, he felt that Joe was unimportant; that he alone was the big man in their mob.

"When Joe's finished I'll make sure you're pleased, Billy," she said, depositing the first pint before him.

Alec Jamison didn't like skinheads. He had good reason for his hatred; his daughter Alice had been raped by one of the bovver boys and the abortion she'd had resulted in an inflammation of the womb which had proved fatal. Now, a gaunt, lonely man with wife and daughter buried in the East London cemetery, Alec listened to the whispered conversation between Billy and Mary.

Alec liked Mary. He knew she was a tramp; available for any man with enough money to double her weekly take from the pub — and that included all her fiddles, too! He didn't care about fiddles… he got enough on the side from his milk round. He didn't give a shit whether she got into bed with her old man or some kid. His women on the round often paid with a bit and he didn't think any less of them for opening their legs.

But, somehow, he couldn't associate Mary with those little bastards in Joe Hawkins' mob. God, how he detested them!

He felt his glass almost creak as his grip tightened…

Then suddenly…

Mary gasped, hand fluttering to her open mouth as blood spurted from Alec's hand. The bitter spilled over the floor, glass shards flying willy-nilly, some sticking from the cut and bleeding palm.

It wasn't so much the shock of seeing Alec smash the glass in his fist; it was his expression — the wild-glaring eyes, the contorted features as he fixed Billy with his demented gaze.

She felt her knees turn rubbery. Alec wasn't the type of man anyone annoyed. Tall, heavy, with the face of an ex-boxer, he looked every inch the determined fighter he certainly was. She'd seen him in action; seen him beat a man to pulp before he recovered his temper. And she feared for Billy...

Glass stabbed into his flesh but he refused to be put off. The bastard had it coming to him and he clenched his fist into a hard-knuckled ball. All the pent-up loathing surged to the surface.

Before he could strike a blow, he felt the sickening weight of a hard object descend on his head... saw dim, flying lights circle the bar and heard the savage cry of one of the young thugs...

Semi-conscious, he felt boots seek his secret places... find them with excruciating thuds... and, as the boots kept going in, the pain lessened... lessened... grew more distant, less brutal!

# CHAPTER FIVE

JOE FLUNG the bedclothes aside with disgust. His body ached – especially where that rotten bastard had planted three darts in his arse. He could still hear the burly man's yell: "I got 'im... treble arse!"

He staggered to his small mirror and looked at his naked image. Christ, he thought, that thing should have been giving Mary a good go last night. If only Billy hadn't been stupid enough to get into bovver with Crazy Alec!

He grinned at his reflection. If he looked terrible Billy must be one awful mess. He'd clobbered Alec before his bloody fist could flatten Billy but that hadn't saved his mate from the ire of those others kindly disposed to Alec. He'd been bleedin' lucky to skip out with but a few fists shoved down his throat. Not Billy! The last he saw, Billy was sprawled on the pub floor getting the dockers' boots rammed home where it would do his sex life most harm. Mary must have gone without from all of them, he mused happily. If he was sure her old man wasn't home he'd go round there and give her what she wanted most!

In his chest of drawers he had some of those Swedish magazines – the type showing pubic hair and highly erotic positional poses between men and women. He got two out, turned to well-thumbed pages and studied a luscious blonde doing a wonderful thing for an unseen male with a tremendous urge for her; to a brunette climbing all over a dark-haired youth whose intentions could not be more obvious.

"Christ..." He flung the magazines back in the drawer and covered them with dirty underwear. Sweat filmed his forehead. He dressed quickly, wearing his skin-tight Levi's so that his boots could be seen in all their savage glory, a skimpy granddad short-sleeved vest and draped a cheap sheepskin around him. Then he gave his boots a fast polish, slipped his feet into them and immediately felt two feet taller. Funny, he thought, lacing the boots, how they gave a guy a boost!

He didn't bother saying good-morning to his parents. They would rave about last night and the blood-stained towel hanging in the bathroom...

Jeeze, that was a laugh! Bathroom... a pokey room with a built-in tin bath and a cracked basin. Even the bloody loo was ready to fall apart. When he got recognized...

One thing Joe really detested was a hippie. For a start, they didn't wash. Then there was the matter of their hair... so bleedin' long and matted with lice and dirt. And their clothes – well, he couldn't bear to rub against one of them anywhere! He always got the shivers thinking of fleas and filth and the sickening stench of unclean material.

Mostly, though, he hated them for not working. He had to work; if he didn't there'd be no cash in pocket. His father was hard when it came to earning money; like most men who had to slave since their early teens to make ends meet. But not the hippies! Not those bastards! The bleedin' Welfare State took care of them – grants if they were students (and that was a big laugh!), handouts from Social Security to pay fines for demonstrating and pot-taking, additional cash to buy more pot and, if they were really lucky to get a sympathetic guy at the Assistance Board, they'd have enough to take a holiday in Cornwall. Christ, what a rotten way to treat tax-payers he thought!

Well, today, they'd do a few hippies for the hell of it. After last night he wanted some easy aggro. No hefty dockers, no bleedin' crazy fools... just soft, dirty hippies to bash around.

Don Taylor tightened his clip-on braces and gazed in admiration at his brand-new Dr. Martens' boots. At ninety-five shillings they were a bargain in his estimation. Like Joe, he felt taller, more important when he wore boots. "It'll be bleedin' cold in Brighton, Joe," he said.

"We'll find a few hairies and get warm doin' them," came the reply.

"I dunno," Don muttered, looking away as Joe's hard eyes fastened on him. "Those Brighton fuzz are hard, man."

Billy nodded agreement. He ached awful and his face looked as though it had gone through a sausage-mixer. He certainly wasn't in the mood to risk another beating so shortly after last night.

"You gettin' yellow?" Joe asked menacingly.

Don shook his head fast. Billy took longer but again agreed.

"Okay then," Joe said firmly. "That's settled. We're goin' to Brighton. Let's get the others..." He strutted off, sure of his men now – a commander about to prepare an attack on an undefended town; a brutal Napoleon ready to strike with all the viciousness of his power-mad soul.

Once they reached Victoria Station, the mob were unanimous about what they intended doing in the seaside town. The proceeds of a small robbery they had pulled the week before would provide their fares, meals and booze. And, when they ran out of amusements, they would seek out a few scared hippies and do them.

The first train was The Pullman and Joe gave his orders: "No bleedin' trouble on this train, mates. We wanna get to Brighton – not arrested."

As they strolled along the platform, the guard eyed them suspiciously. He didn't enjoy having yobbos on his train; no more than the nervous passengers watching from carriage windows wanted them in their compartments. But Joe wasn't interested in annoying innocent travellers today. He was thinking about what would happen once they cornered their hippie enemies and enjoyed the prospect of putting his boot in.

"'Ere's one…" Billy pointed at a carriage where several teenage girls sat watching their progress along the cold-swept platform.

"Christ, can't you think of sumfin' besides girls?"

Billy shrugged, and waved to the stern-faced females. Joe wasn't usually so slow at taking opportunities. If he stayed in this mood they'd have a lousy day by the sea.

It wasn't often Joe felt compelled to explain his edicts, but he did, loudly: "We get in there an' there'll be bovver for sure. I don't want anyfing to stop us doin' them hippies." He smiled, shaking himself like some huge bear about to itch against a benevolent tree-trunk. "After yesterday we're not goin' to have our sport spoilt."

Billy grinned happily. He, too, wanted to gain a measure of sweat revenge for the beating he'd taken trying to make Mary. But he also wanted a bird. The long hours contemplating how it would be with Mary had given him the urge. And all the boots, fists and broken bottles that had found their target in his flesh hadn't dulled his massive desire. If only Joe would let them combine pleasures...

"Ain't we gonna chat-up any birds, Joe?"

Joe shrugged, throwing open a carriage door. "Mebbe *after* the aggro, Don. Get in..." He stalked down the carriage, taking a window seat. One elderly man at the far end of the carriage glanced fearfully over his Sunday newspaper and hurriedly buried his nose in the latest scandal. Like so many people he figured that what he couldn't see wouldn't come to lay grief on his doorstep.

"'Ow much we got, Joe?"

Billy rubbed his hands together, waiting for Joe's reply to Tony's pertinent question. He hoped it would be enough for them to make steak and chips – not the old standard fish with.

"Thirty knicker."

"Cor, we bleedin' well nicked over sixty-five!"

"Yeah," Joe said softly. "An' I divvied out some."

Tony dropped his gaze and sulked in his corner. He didn't dare query Joe further. He knew – as did the others – that Joe had taken a larger slice than any of them. He always did. As their leader he apportioned the spoils and, with deference to his superior position, allotted himself the general's ration.

Slowly at first, then gathering speed, the train moved out of the station, the crumbling warehouses and dilapidated homes along the track like sickness on the face of London. Joe didn't see the horror of railway surroundings. Nothing here was worse than his own neighbourhood; nothing dirtier than Plaistow or Poplar. Although he had ambitions to rise above the filth of working class districts, he had accepted conditions with the fatalism of those born to squalor. It was one thing to believe in a West End flat, a Mayfair bird, a gleaming car and new gear every day of the week, but the brainwashed mind could not see further than personal betterment. It couldn't realise that all of this slumland must be cleared and kept free from decay. It couldn't accept that people had to be educated to have pride in their surroundings, to make their district forever clean and fresh and on a par with other high-class areas.

As the train sped past a huge new office building near the Thames with its huge red sign announcing space to let, Joe felt a tremor of annoyance. From the top floor of that block, one would see across the river to the Houses of Parliament, down river, up river, see all the landmarks of the city. He had a fair idea what a flat there would cost always providing the landlords would rent to a private individual instead of a large company.

That was the closest Joe came to speculating on his future residential ambitions that day. For the most of the fast journey he allowed himself the luxury of imagining how they – the mob – would deal with his hated hippies.

Basically, Joe had a feeling for violence. It was an integral part of his make-up. Some do-gooders trying to explain his attachment to the skinhead cult would, no doubt, stress his environmental background, his childhood fighting for every scrap of education and clothing. They would point with undisguised delight to his father's tough profession, to the East End as a breeding-ground of crime and the conditions under which its inhabitants grew up. They would gleefully assign all manner of reasons for Joe being what he was without ever touching on the most important factor of all – his character weakness for brutality. It wasn't something that had grown inside him because of surrounding blights. It was him; he was one of the incurables – one of those born to be hard, mean, savage. Nothing had made Joe this. He had been born to accept crime and the ravaging of that which he found objectionable. Joe Hawkins was one of nature's misfits; one of her habitual criminals. And all the soft-soap and kindness would not alter him. Not one iota.

# CHAPTER SIX

"Jesus, Don – you're a stupid bastard!"

Don laughed, dug his hands deeper into his pockets. It was freezing cold along the front and the wind-whipped waves formed salting white-caps as far into the Channel as the eye could see. "Relax, Joe-mate... they didn't get us, did they?"

Joe growled into his sheepskin coat, feeling his face getting numb as the wind continued to assault them. "They bleedin' nearly did, you bastard! If it hadn't been for Billy..."

Billy turned his back on the spray blowing over the sea-wall, hearing the incessant rattle of pebbles under the smashing waves. It had been bloody close, he thought walking backwards. They'd slashed the seats and bust a carriage window just as the train was entering Brighton Station but Don had to act the fool and throw light-bulbs onto the platform. If he hadn't run to the copper and made a complaint about a mythical member of the Hell's Angel's mob going for him, Don would be freezing his arse inside a Brighton cell now. "Fuckin' fool!" Billy said as the wind tore his words away and rushed them down to the marina.

"Let's eat, Joe," Tony voiced, glaring at the angry sea. "I'm starvin'."

Joe nodded. He was hungry too. And he didn't much fancy being blown to bits any longer. They'd seen the bleedin' sea and, for his money, Brighton could keep it. He didn't go much on sand and sea and sky. He preferred the city with its layers of smoke blotting out the sun, with its teeming millions struggling for a mere existence, for the aggro and for the clash of wills.

The caff catered to early holiday-makers but on a cold, lonely Sunday it was practically empty. The menu didn't offer much in the way of good eating but Joe wasn't one to know the intricacies of *Cordon Bleu* cuisine. His idea of a slap-up meal consisted of chips with everything and a steak could be raw, medium or burnt to a crisp for all the difference it made to his cast-iron stomach. He had no real sense of taste – a result of years spent eating his mother's cooking. In the Hawkins' household a chop tasted like fish and fish tasted like rubberized shoe leather. Nobody would ever honour Mrs. Hawkins for her cooking. Nobody!

"Listen sonny... I don't want any trouble, hear me?"

Joe grinned at the swarthy, heavy-set man behind the counter. He had a feeling the out-of-sight right hand was lovingly caressing a truncheon. He didn't want trouble then either. Especially not with a typical East Ender operating a profitable Brighton caff.

"Isn't it the shits!" Joe said in a low voice, "'ere we are in dear old Brighton an' he slaps a law on us already!" He laughed, motioned for the mob to take their seats, bending forward and telling the owner in a confidential whisper: "Mate we're famished – we wanna eat... okay?"

"Just remember," the other growled, "no trouble. You pays when I bring the nosh!"

"Suit yourself, chief," Joe replied in his most casual manner. "Wot's your tip for the day?"

"Ham san'ich."

"Christ, I said we're bleedin' famished..."

"You got money?" the owner asked suspiciously remembering other skinheads and other non-payment of bills.

Joe deliberately withdrew his cash, flicked the fivers to prove his intention to pay. Inside, he boiled. It would serve the bastard right if they done his place and didn't pay. But he controlled his emotions and forced a smile. "'Ow's that?"

"Right... What's the order?"

As Joe took his seat, Billy leant forward and snarled, "Let's do the bastard when he brings the nosh."

Joe considered the request, but brushed it aside. His plans were swiftly formulating. First, they'd find a few hippies and kick the shit out of them. Secondly they'd run riot in whatever amusement arcades were open. Thirdly, they'd come back here and bust the caff's windows and, if they could, break every stick of furniture in the rotten place. Maybe they'd even have the satisfaction of doing the owner. That would make the current backing down worthwhile.

"No, Billy," he said finally. "Save 'im for later." He winked, letting them all know he – their supreme commander – had a definite scheme afoot.

"Let's have the most expensive nosh, eh?" Don said with a sly grin. "We can always get our money back... *later*!"

Joe nodded, wondering if his plan would let them rob the geezer. He doubted if an East Ender would leave his spare cash lying around where yobbos could find it. He wouldn't... and he placed the owner in this category.

Without exception, the mob followed Joe's selection from the hand-scrawled menu: soup, minute steak with boiled potatoes and peas, cheese and biscuits, tea.

None of them complained when the soup arrived lukewarm. Nobody noticed that the minute steak was tough, sinewy, an unfrozen offering to nauseate a gourmet, and that the potatoes were a day old and reheated. None of them paid any attention to the tinned peas and the way they came up in solid balls. And even the cheese passed their non-inspection although it smelt to high heaven and had mould on the edges. As for the biscuits the least said about them the better.

Only one item on the menu passed for what it said – the tea. It was hot, fresh, sweet.

"Like it?" the owner asked with a secret smile as Joe again withdrew his cash.

"Not bad!"

Money exchanged hands – an exorbitant amount duly paid without a query.

As the mob trooped from the caff, the owner laughed and muttered to himself, "Bleedin' fools!" Then leaving just enough change in the till, he folded his notes, placed them in a paper bag, put that inside an open packet of Tate & Lyle sugar and left it in plain sight on a shelf. Ringing up NO SALE he removed five shillings, put in a seven-sided atrocity which decimalisation had decided to thrust upon an unwilling public and helped himself to a packet of Everest cigarettes. As he lit one he watched the mob stagger down the front, the wind in their faces. "Bleedin' fools!" he said aloud and blew a smoke ring with expert ease...

"I feel full up," Don bucked the steadily rising gale, the remains of his meal resting like lead balls in his stomach.

"Let's have a few beers, Joe," Tony suggested.

"Yeah, that's an idea," Billy agreed.

Joe cut around the bus depot and past the dolphin statue. He knew a large pub where they could get served without the fuzz noticing they were in town. It made him feel good to exhibit himself in a conspicuous place like the pub he had in mind. Almost like those Western movies he avidly watched on the goggle-box. He pictured himself as the villain going into a strange town, ready to meet any challenge, prepared to face up to the marshall.

"Christ!" Billy examined the pub's interior with awe. He was used to East End establishments with their smaller bars, their dinginess. He hadn't expected Joe to select such an opulent tavern. He had never before seen such grandeur – unless one counted the time his school paid a visit to Hampton Court Palace. He had been seven then and his memory could still conjure up images of the vastness of those rooms, the armorial bearings and the instruments of torment with which the ancient men attacked their foes.

Joe stalked to the bar giving the snooty barmaid a wink and getting a haughty look in return. He knew the score – his kind were unwelcome in these hallowed precincts. But he didn't flinch. He ordered beer, flashed a fiver, and waited for the slow service which said more than any retort could have.

A log fire burned in a huge hearth, expensively dressed people chatted quietly and, across the room two young birds got their heads together and their legs further apart as Joe's mob swilled their beer.

"l can see 'er knickers," Don enthused.

"Bloody hell... 'er mate ain't wearin' any." Billy almost jumped from his seat, only to have Joe restrain him.

"Not in 'ere," Joe snarled.

"But, Joe... she's..."

"I said..."

"Okay, Joe!" Billy controlled himself, refusing to take his eyes from the delightful view of the girl with her thighs spread wide apart.

"I'd like to start a fight in 'ere," Don remarked with relish.

"Me too," Tony chipped in.

"I'd like to fuck that bird!" Billy said eagerly.

Joe scowled, finished his brew. "Let's find the hippies."

"Naw, let's have another..."

Joe turned on Billy. "I said – let's go!"

Billy drank his beer, wiped his lips, leered at the girls and followed Joe from the pub. On the street he glanced around. "There ain't goin' to be hippies out in this."

"If we walk towards Roedean we'll find 'em," Joe said with authority.

Don laughed to himself and finally said, "My old man used to tell us about the time he was stationed down 'ere durin' the war. They was in Roedean an' they 'ad a notice on the gates sayin' RING FOR A MISTRESS..." His laughter erupted anew; a lonely laugh the others failed to appreciate. Perhaps it was the way he told it.

"I'd like a bleedin' mistress now," Billy said hopefully.

"Me too," Tony quipped. He glanced at Joe. "'Ow about it, mate. Can't we find a coupla birds an'..."

"After we find a few hippies!" Joe remarked adamantly.

He was consumed with hatred and anxiety. What if, he found himself thinking, they didn't locate any hippies? What would they do then? His leadership depended on getting the boot in.

They walked along the spray-swept front, past the marina, the motor museum, the rows of cold, unfriendly houses perched high on the hill. Hotel signs glowed faintly in the greying sky, offering some warmth and companionship behind their bland facades.

Out to sea, tossed as a cork in a violently disturbed bathtub, a small coastal vessel battled the frothed waves. When the breakers swooshed up the shore, row-boats rattled and shifted at anchor. And, always, there was the restless sound of stone under water as the sea rearranged the composition of the beach once again.

"It's bloody cold!" Billy wasn't thinking of birds now. The biting wind had long since whipped away desire, leaving him wishing for the warmth of a log fire and the sanctuary of a pub.

Up ahead, where their paths rose to meet the road to Hastings, a small group of figures detached themselves from a shelter and started walking down to the beach. Joe stiffened. Even at that distance he could see long hair caught in the freezing wind and could make out gear that wasn't worn by ordinary people.

He grunted, rubbing his hands together in anticipation. "Hairies!" he snarled.

Billy yelled and felt for his tool. The coldness of metal did not shock him; his senses were attuned to violence and the thought of laying into a bleedin' hippie made him feel suddenly hot.

Don and Tony too, had withdrawn their crude clubs – Don's had once been an axe handle while Tony believed in using a tyre iron cut down to right size in Ford's workshops.

Joe didn't have a weapon. He'd come to Brighton for the pleasure of kicking hippies – not bustin' their skulls with a tool. His boots were weaponry enough and, anyway, he wanted the satisfaction of feeling his toe sink in deep.

"Don't let 'em see we're looking for aggro," Joe warned. "Let it be a surprise, eh?"

From their vantage point, the five hippies saw the others approaching. They were cold, hungry, unafraid. They didn't consider an attack on a day like this as even a remote possibility. That they had roughed it for the last week didn't mean their natural enemies – skinheads and Hell's Angels – would brave the bitter weather and venture to Brighton's storm-tossed icebox.

It was afternoon and the last meal they'd been able to cadge had been in Eastbourne the previous night. They had some pot left, some cigarettes and tomorrow, Monday, the Social Security office would give them enough to take care of immediate problems.

"Turn back, Roger..."

Roger was a tall man with flowing dark hair and a small beard. His mandarin moustache had never quite succeeded in becoming Chinese and formed a wispy coating above firm lips. "What's wrong, Cherry?" he asked, unable to comprehend her.

"I don't like the look of those boys," The girl replied, fear suddenly tugging at her heart. She was only eighteen but she had had enough experience fighting off those who wished to destroy them. She had taken part in practically every demonstration in Grosvenor Square, been arrested sixteen times for obstruction or disturbing the peace and, always without exception, had the Welfare State pay her fine. She had had two abortions on the State, been in receipt of a student grant until she tired of her fellow students using her as a physical oil-change. Since meeting Roger she had wandered from one end of the country to another, sleeping rough, eating when they could, stealing a little here and there to pay for pot and, when they found a sympathetic Civil Servant, begging a pitiful sum from the tax payers to let them continue the anti-social life they insisted was right.

She was a pretty girl beneath the grime of their outdoor existence; a girl with a high I.Q. gone to "pot". She liked calling herself that. It amused her to watch intelligent faces light up and acknowledge her witticism.

"Cherry's right, Rog," Joel Standish said calmly. His American accent bit into the wind. "They're coming after us!" For himself, he didn't give a goddam what happened. He was sick and needed hospitalization anyway. His ulcers were reaching danger point. In a way, he'd welcome a beating and deportation. He could think of better places to go hippie than England. He thought about California and the communes; about the searing head of Death Valley and the wild life the likes of a Manson could have there. He thought about orgies where the girls were all naked and the pot was freshly imported from Mexico and the desert sun beat down to provide a love nest of shifting hot sand.

Then, suddenly, he thought about his draft dodging and how they'd grab him and toss him into a hoosegow once he set foot in Uncle Sam's land. Fear clogged his nostrils. "Let's get the hell away from here, Rog," he yelled, turning to run.

"No..."

Roger was too late. The moment Joel turned tail, Joe and his mob broke into a run.

Cherry screamed, threw herself over a low fence and rolled down the incline, her sleeping bag denting her soft side as she rolled over and over.

He couldn't tell it was a girl trying to escape. He jumped the fence, slithered down the steep incline and landed on top of her as she sprawled on the pebble beach. His tool rose ready to smash down on the unprotected head until he saw her face.

Slowly, he lowered his hand, ripped her duffle coat open and felt for her breasts.

"You bastard!" she screamed up at him.

Billy felt the old urge return as he squeezed soft yielding flesh. His hand worked inside her jeans down... down, until he felt her pubic hair. "Christ, I'm goin' to rape you," he mouthed.

Cherry fought. She didn't mind the act itself but she objected to being used in plain sight of these animals. His hand was hurting her, his fingers exploring without regard for the tenderness of her body. Her fist smashed into his face... into the damage of last night. He yelled, his tool catching her a hard blow above the eye. She slumped dazed, shocked, unable to resist his frantic attempts to rip her jeans off.

Joe felt his boot sink deep into the tall one's groin. He lashed out again, catching the other under the chin as he sank to the ground, hands clutching the injured parts. Like an automaton, Joe kept kicking... each blow bringing him greatest satisfaction as the moans of hurt rose above the screaming wind. He didn't care if he killed the hippie or not. He wanted to hurt... to rid himself of the feeling within his chest; a feeling bordering on murderous rage.

Don laughed, slammed his shortened axe handle almost down the hippie's throat as the man valiantly tried to resist. It was easy, Don thought, kicking his opponent in the balls, listening to the rapturous sigh, the explosive groan. He hit the falling hippie on the head, hearing the crunch of bone against axe handle, and kicked into the ribs.

Tony watched blood flow from the ripped head of his target. That made two for him. The other wasn't moving now. A few fast belts with his tool and several well aimed kicks had taken care of him. He glanced down the incline, saw Billy mounting the girl, and yelled joyously. He kicked his second opponent in the face, slammed the tyre iron down on the bloody head again and vaulted the fence.

"Me next, mate," he yelled, watching Billy penetrate the half-stupefied girl hippie. Her jeans lay on the beach, her thighs pimpled with cold, her buttocks bruised by the relentless rocks that formed this section of the shoreline.

Joe wanted to keep kicking the hippie but, somehow the pleasure had ebbed since the other ceased to fight back; since the unresisting body had stopped moving. He turned away in disgust to seek another fresh target for his rage.

"Bloody fools," he yelled, catching sight of Billy and Tony. He glanced down the road, saw a familiar car starting to enter it from the direction of the marina. He jumped the fence and raced downhill. "Get out of the bitch!" he hollered at Billy, tearing his mate from the girl's nakedness. "Fuzz..."

"I ain't finished it yet," Billy wailed, eyes wild and staring at her nudity. God how he loved thick pubic hair! She had the thickest covering of any bird he'd ever stripped.

"You'll be finished if the fuzz get you," Joe snapped. "Come on – run!" He started running along the beach, seeing Don slither and fall as he followed in their wake. He didn't care if Billy had to run with it out – that was his fault for trying to do two things at once!

*

The train took its time leaving the station. Joe felt on edge, seated at the window, straining to see if the fuzz were coming down the platform. At last, as the wheels began to catch, he breathed a sigh of relief.

"Bleedin' lucky, mate," he told Billy. He saw Preston Park flash past as the train gathered speed. "Christ, can't you ever go on an aggro without trying to find a bird to fuck?"

Billy sulked. He felt worse than he had earlier. He had a bad case of "lover's balls". If only Joe had let him have just another couple of plunges…

"Did you see it, Joe?" Tony asked.

"Yeah, so wot… she's no different from other birds."

"Jeeze, she had…"

"Shuddup," Billy growled. "I know wot she 'ad."

Joe grinned. He'd expended his hatred. Now, he could afford to vent a little spite on Billy. "Tell me about 'er, Tony," he said deliberately. "Was she hairy…?"

Billy tried to close his ears as Tony delighted in describing the girl in intimate detail. He couldn't help overhearing how Tony had viewed his hasty mating nor how he had looked when Joe dragged him off the bitch. He wished the fuzz had caught the others and let him finish. He'd have to find a bird when they got back to Plaistow or else he'd have an awful night of it again...

# CHAPTER SEVEN

FOR FOUR DAYS of every week Joe worked for a coal delivery merchant. He never worked a Tuesday, but that was tomorrow and his reasons did not bear thinking about until...

He hated Monday almost as much as he hates hippies. He had read the *Mirror*'s account of the young thugs who had viciously attacked five hippies in Brighton and tried to mass-rape the girl with them. He had read, with a high degree of pleasure, how the four male hippies were in serious condition in Brighton hospital and that the girl had been released after getting stitches in a head wound. Fortunately, the description issued by the police would fit any skinhead in London so he didn't think they'd ever trace the mob from Brighton.

His mate on the delivery lorry was a man of about forty – an illiterate Cockney with a fantastic sense of humour but nothing else to qualify him as Joe's mate. Joe worked his fiddles with a recklessness that increased the thrill of robbing old age pensioners and old women too timid to object to his overcharging. He had a standard method of getting a few bob from every customer – he simply altered their half of the delivery slip to read a higher amount. If they argued, which was seldom, he argued back – and usually won. If they threatened to telephone the company he'd back down with a grin and explain that some stupid bastard of a clerk had made a mistake.

There were a few calls where fiddles were strictly *verboten* – like when they had a delivery to Mrs. Marrinor. He always let his mate heave the coal into her basement. And, naturally enough, he never appeared again until he had satisfied the middle-aged nympho's craving for a "dirty coalman to jump on top of my lily-white flesh".

Oh, there were perks galore for delivering coal!

Another non-fiddle place of call was on the estate. Mrs. "bleedin' heart" Bassault, the French bird whose husband always seemed to be away on some ship or another. Joe knew all about her. She was the Point professional fuck. Any man with enough ready cash left after a night in the local boozer could stop off at her flat to avail himself of her excellent services regardless of whether or not he could, or could not, perform with a skinful on. Mrs. Bassault had never been known to fail when she was paid for relieving frustrations. One way – or another – she guaranteed results.

This Monday they had six bags for Mrs. Bassault.

"Look, mate," Joe told his driver, "she's due for it. Let me 'ave it today?"

The older man screwed his piggish eyes into slits and considered Joe's request. He had been thinking how nice it would be for himself. He hadn't been getting his share off the old woman for weeks and he was overdue to make a personal delivery to Mrs. Bassault's bedroom. "I dunno..." he said.

"A quid if you let me..."

"Shit! I'd pay twice that to call at night."

"Okay, two quid!" Joe felt generous. He'd made forty-seven shillings that morning already. And, he had what was left of the robbery in his wallet, too.

"Done! Ram her for me, eh?" the driver chuckled as he eased his lorry into the Point driveway and parked directly behind the Bassault block.

Mrs. Bassault didn't question Joe's urgent knocks. She looked at him and said, "Coal today?" She stood back and added, "I'm short of cash but..." Her robe fell open displaying knickers and brassiere and expanses of creamy flesh.

Joe crudely pulled the front of her knickers down and studied the pubic region. "Sorry, Mrs. Bassault

– we're short on cash this week. I'm afraid I can only deduct a quid…"

"You're a *big* boy," she replied. "I suppose…" She moved away as the coal-dust on his hand left a black mark down her gently-rounded stomach. Where his fingers had gripped her pink knickers the individual black prints showed too. She glared at these, and said testily, "I hate washing them, Joe."

"Take everything off," he said, starting to unzip his flies. "I won't dirty your bed today, either. The floor's great."

She spread newspaper on the carpet, stripped and lay back with her thighs wide apart. Her hands came up, and out. "Don't keep me waiting, Joe…"

*

"Was it good?"

Joe inclined his head. "Like it always is… in, out, up, down and thanks for bringing the coal, Joe."

"We've got Sally Vincent today," the man said slowly, watching Joe's face.

Joe cursed. He should have studied the delivery sheet. If he'd known Sally was one of their customers he'd have let this bastard fuck the French whore.

"I get 'er, eh Joe?"

"Yeah, you get Sally!"

After he heaved the coal down Sally's chute he returned to the lorry and sweated out the half-hour before his mate returned. His imagination ran riot thinking of Sally. He knew exactly what would happen inside her house... he'd been through the procedure often enough to visualize her performance. She didn't believe in intercourse in the ordinary way. She didn't want a bastard, she always said. She had her own pleasurable method for making her delivery men pay for her creature-comforts. The milkman for one, got his treatment every Monday. The laundryman got his on Friday. The gas and electricity blokes always came away swearing she had been a frugal customer. And, whenever she wanted coal, she got a delivery and a forty-five minute thrill. Not to mention what the coalman got.

"Hey, Joe... she let me into 'er..."

Joe felt sick. Ever since he took this flamin' job he'd wanted into Sally. Now, this old bastard had done the bit.

"She was pissed," his mate kept saying. "Pissed! Seems she discovered her old man put one in her oven and she don't give a cunt anymore!" The driver chuckled, got behind the steering-wheel. "Cor, she did give me one! I tell you – there ain't no woman with a better set or a more active..."

"For chrissakes, dry up!" Joe shouted.

He felt so rotten he didn't even attempt to argue when an old age pensioner contested his charges. He changed her figures back to normal, stamped off to the lorry and growled for his mate to hurry. For once, the Cockney humour was lacking. His mate didn't wish to rile Joe. He'd have ample opportunity to sleep in a cold bed that night and cogitate over his earlier success.

*

The church basement was crowded with clean, respectable teenagers. They were enjoying their weekly social and the vicar kept changing the discs and serving the coffee without one single word of discouragement.

They were an exuberant crowd, perfectly content in the knowledge that St. James's was a church young people could be proud of, and assured of a weekly welcome from the with-it vicar.

Every Sunday, the church was able to boast of superlative attendances — mostly consisting of teenager adherents to the open policies that had initiated their decorous youth club.

Peter Bloomfield studied the group dancing and inwardly congratulated himself for the success he had had with what had always been classified an unruly element in his district. In his opinion, God was not a harsh God, nor an authoritarian. God was love and love should be that emotion shared with one's fellow man or woman (always depending, naturally, on the holy state of matrimony; he did not condone the permissiveness that certain elements of society tried to force churchmen into accepting).

"How are things at home, Albert?" he asked as a tall, thin youngster came to stand beside him.

Albert Newton shrugged casually. He wasn't one of those who accepted Bloomfield as the "teenager's saviour". He had his reservations and, mostly, they revolved around the vicar's pet theory that sex before marriage was illicit, immoral, bad for a "God-blessed" union. Albert was virile and could always get any girl he went after. He enjoyed feeling around and exercising his manhood. For that reason he was the blackest sheep in the vicar's little fold.

"Not bad, Mr. Bloomfield," he replied, conscious of the need to treat the man with a certain respect. He didn't realise that it was this deference that made him Bloomfield's special target. In the vicar's mind, any teenager willing to show respect was worth saving.

"Has your father found a job yet?"

Albert grunted. "How could he?"

There was no answer to that, Bloomfield thought. Mr. Newton was one of nature's favourite layabouts. He had feigned illness so long he would not know how to find the strength to go for an interview.

"I see Betty Rowe is here tonight..."

Albert tightened up inside.

"She asked if you were coming..."

Albert lit a cigarette.

"Have you thought about what I suggested the last time we met?"

The boy grinned. "Yeah. No!"

Peter Bloomfield felt the immediate urge to rant at the youth. He calmed himself and said: "There's nothing wrong with being a police constable, Albert."

"No?" Albert savagely stubbed his cigarette into the palm of one hand – a feat he had perfected since seeing it done on television by a so-called hard man. "They're underpaid, nobody likes 'em and I don't want my head kicked in at demos..."

"Ah," the vicar smiled, placing a hand on the boy's shoulder. "I see." He didn't really! "You think all policemen spend their time getting maltreated?"

"Don't they?" Albert wanted to hurt. Ever since the vicar had suggested he join the force he had seriously tried to get his inner-self to agree. He liked the idea of walking round his district in a nice blue uniform. He enjoyed the prospect – imaginary, of course – of apprehending villains. Yet, he couldn't go against public opinion and his mates.

"What I had in mind," the vicar continued with his infectious enthusiasm, "was a course at a police college. None of the beat pounding trivia for you, Albert. I have funds at my disposal. The Church would provide a grant to see you through the course..." His face broke into a benevolent smile and his eyes searched through Albert – almost to the closed soul-door.

Albert hesitated. He wanted to accept – on the spot. He wanted to tell this man that he was the best person he had ever met... and couldn't. His upbringing forbade any emotional response. His father's constant claims that the State owed its citizens a living, that nobody got anywhere offering their services stuck in his mind; and in his heart.

"I tell you, Joe – they've got birds in there would turn your head," Billy remarked as they lounged outside the church hall.

"Wot's keepin' us from getting a few?" Don asked.

Joe scowled. He'd had his bit for the day and tomorrow was Tuesday. He had to keep reasonably virile for Tuesday! "Christ – you wanna go in?" he asked sulkily.

"Yeah!"

"Okay..." Joe shoved the door open and faced a frightened goody-goody boy. "Move aside, pansy," Joe shouted, shoving the boy over amid a collection of flying tickets.

For a moment, nobody noticed their arrival. Then, when Billy grabbed one of the girls, a scream split the hall into factions and Joe's mob found themselves confronted by hostile glares. Just glares. Nothing else.

"Keep dancin'," Joe announced. "We ain't goin' to rape you bleedin' virgins." He grinned and added in a stage-whisper to Billy, "Are we?"

"I bloody-well am," Billy said in a loud voice. "That one over there!" He indicated a girl of about fifteen wearing a mini and a tight blouse. Billy took a step towards the girl...

"Just a moment!" Peter Bloomfield tried to control his seething anger. First, he turned the record player off, then he walked through the parting crowd of his flock and stood facing Joe Hawkins. He recognised Joe; knew that this was the most serious crisis ever to be thrust upon his small gathering. Joe represented evil; Lucifer in clip-on braces and wearing devilish boots.

Joe laughed and touched Don's arm. "Get a load of 'im," he clowned, affecting the vicar's mode of walk.

"You bastard!"

Joe glanced round the hall, trying to catch sight of the speaker. It certainly didn't *sound* like one of the flock – not using *that* language here.

Albert stepped forward, joining the vicar as a team pitted against a superior side.

Joe felt apprehension race down his spine. He and Albert had attended the same school and the only boy he had never been able to lick was Albert Newton. He recalled several bloody noses and black eyes when he antagonized the same Albert.

"You don't belong here, Joe," Albert said evenly. "Get lost! Go bovver some other function but forget this one!"

Joe forced a scowl intended to frighten his opponent. He *couldn't* back down. Not in front of the mob.

"Please..." Peter Bloomfield smiled at Albert, placing a restraining arm before the youth, and took a tentative step to Joe.

Billy growled, aiming a solid kick at the vicar's groin...

Don whooped, tearing into three timid youngsters near him; his tool flashing, hitting; his boots finding their soft targets without much satisfaction gained.

Before he knew what was happening, Albert lunged forward, slamming a right, left, right into Joe's face. Joe staggered back. Albert closed in, not letting those deadly boots get freedom of movement, his bunched fists pounding into Joe's unprotected middle.

From his undistinguished position on the dusty floor, Peter Bloomfield watched the battle with prayers on his lips. His groin hurt, his hopes pinned on Albert's initiative. If only the others would back Albert...

Albert didn't require backing at this stage. He was hammering Joe into insensibility, driving rights and lefts at the skinhead leader... forcing him back... back... back against a solid wall from which there was no escape.

"That's enough m'lad!" A heavy hand pulled Albert off his enemy.

Joe shook his head, desperately trying to clear the fog that threatened to make him a sitting-bird. He heard the strange voice, saw Albert half-turn away from him and...

"*God!*" Albert sank to his knees as Joe's boot found his stomach. He wanted to be sick... couldn't.

"Little swine!" The stranger slashed a stiff-hand across Joe's throat, sending the skinhead reeling. Then, swinging into action, he vaulted the prostrate Albert, rabbit-punching Billy to his knees before making a flying tackle that brought Don down with a *whump*!

Joe struggled to his feet, his throat raw. Through the mist hanging over the hall he saw Don struggling with the stranger. It wasn't his fight, he reasoned and, sensing the nausea in his guts, he stumbled out of the hall into the fresh air. He was sick in the street, thankful for the fact that none of his mates could see him.

Inside the hall, bedlam reigned...

Don fought back with all the ferocity of his mind. His tool knocked the attacker flat, then, using his boots, he slammed kick after kick into unprotected ribs until the sickening sound of cracking bone told him he'd done enough damage.

Backing away, he helped Billy to his feet, but found his way blocked by Albert.

"I'll kill you, you bastard!" Don snarled, brandishing his tool.

Albert shrugged and moved aside.

Don backed to the door and lumbered by the semi-unconscious Billy, As he pushed the door open, Albert leapt forward, his foot a blur in the subdued lighting of the hall. He felt the toe dig into Don's side and steadied himself for a second kick where it would count.

"Albert... NO!!!"

Albert hesitated, watching Don heave himself through the swinging door with Billy still clutched under one arm.

"Don't let them make you into what *they* are!"

Albert turned slowly. Peter Bloomfield swayed unsteadily before him. The vicar's face was a study of ecstasy and agony.

"Don't, Albert..."

Albert relaxed. The fury was spent. He went to the vicar, supporting him now.

"We'll need men of your calibre," the vicar said through his pain. "Think about what I suggested, Albert..."

"Excuse me, sir..."

Peter Bloomfield turned his attention on the stranger in their midst. Albert eyed the man with outright suspicion. He didn't trust sudden appearances nor did he like what was formulating in his mind. The man smelt like a copper. "I'm a police officer..." The stranger said.

Albert stiffened automatically.

"Do any of you know the men who attacked you?"

Peter Bloomfield smiled wearily. He glanced at Albert, feeling that this was the youth's moment of truth. He said: "Personally, I don't want to press charges, officer."

Albert smiled with his own weariness, too. He was being pressured. He knew it, as sure as he could feel the strength surging back into the vicar. He released the other, taking a few steps away to stand aloof from the interrogation.

"We're trying to encourage teenagers to accept us," the vicar continued. "It wouldn't help our cause to lay a complaint on one specific boy, or girl."

The police officer grunted. "That's where you're wrong, sir. It would help a great deal. These young thugs need to be taught a lesson. A six-month sentence would serve 'em right!"

Albert mentally agreed. Joe Hawkins and his mob needed a dose of prison.

"I disagree, officer," Bloomfield remarked. "They need charity and tolerance..." His gaze swung to encompass Albert now.

The plainclothes man shrugged and turned to leave. "If you happen to remember who they were, sir – get in touch with your local police station...

before they commit murder, sir!" He opened the door and departed with a thought-wish expression.

"Mr. Bloomfield..."

The vicar smiled at Albert.

"I'll take that grant you spoke about!"

Peter Bloomfield held out his hand. Perhaps, he thought, the agony searing his insides was worth-while after all. "I'll make the arrangements, Albert. You'll make a wonderful policeman."

Albert grinned. "That's debatable, sir – but I won't let Joe and his mob get away with what they've done when I'm in uniform..."

# CHAPTER EIGHT

EVERY TUESDAY, Joe left the house as though he was going to work. In actuality, he didn't. Never on Tuesday! Tuesday was his day for a piece... a very special piece.

At Swete Street he almost got clobbered by a taxi-cab and he spent five minutes recovering, blasting passers-by with a violence that frightened off several old biddies going to the Co-op for their shopping. By the time he had passed the station where cabbies gathered looking for fares, he had cooled somewhat. But not enough. He stalked to one cab, thrust his head inside the open side-window, and cursed the driver until the man called for help.

Joe didn't wait for reinforcements to arrive. He knew better. Cabbies in this district could handle themselves – especially when they outnumbered the opposition!

He was feeling big when he arrived at *her* house.

Every Tuesday, her mother went shopping – not locally as most women hereabouts did, but to Ilford where bargains could be found and the larger stores offered a greater variety of goods for the housewife.

"Joe..." she hissed as she opened the front door.

"Christ, Sally..." He stepped inside, feeling her hot tongue probing his mouth, her hands feverishly unzipping his flies.

"Oh, Joe..."

"Can't you bleedin' wait?"

"No, Joe... feel me!"

He felt her breasts with their hard-tipped response arousing him immediately. He felt lower, between her thighs getting the same urgent reaction.

"Joe... Hurry..."

He rushed her along the short, narrow hall, feeling the almost impossible *hurry* she insisted upon. They were practically naked when they reached her cramped room – her abject surrender evident when she flung herself on the unmade bed and opened her legs wide.

He flung his clothes across the room, unable to tear his gaze from where her hand rested... agitating herself into acceptance of what was about to happen.

"Joe..." She held her arms out, shuddering as she saw his nudity.

He fell on her, fumbling for contact...

"Joe..." she wailed as he inserted his penis. Then as he continued to plunge up and down on her, she gave herself totally to his frantic pleasure... gyrating; moaning; begging him to go faster...

"Okay?" he asked, rolling from her.

"Joe..." Tears stung her eyes. It had been beautiful. What she wanted from him every night of the week; what she couldn't have because her father forbade her to associate with a bastard like Joe.

"Let's have a kip."

She snuggled against his naked chest. Her hand fondled him, loving the slickness of what had recently been her passion. "Marry me, Joe."

He stiffened. "You're crazy, Sally. We ain't old enough."

"I'd run away with you, Joe..."

"Christ," he exploded. "You're fourteen, Sally!"

"And I take the Pill so you can..."

"Jeeze, I know, doll."

"Don't that mean somethin'?"

"Yeah, crawl over me. I'm getting the urge again..."

Her body flowed through his greedy hands, her thighs straddling him.

"Cor..." He kissed a breast, hands actively working between her thighs.

She bent over him, positioning herself… all fourteen years of experience doing what came naturally on their Tuesday.

"I'm ready," Joe whispered…

She sank onto him, loving the feeling of his penis buried in her body.

# CHAPTER NINE

"It was lovely, Joe." She lay by his side, her hand toying with his genitals.

He felt sleepy. Funny, he thought, how he wanted to sleep after a good screw. "That's terrific," he growled, twisting on one side.

"Joe...?"

"Yeah!"

"Can't we run away an' get married?"

"No!"

"Why not? Others do..."

"You're only fourteen."

"So what? I can take everything you've got, can't I?"

"When I'm ready to give, doll," he rasped.

She giggled playing with him. "It won't take long, Joe 'awkins."

"Crissakes, you've 'ad it twice already."

"So what?" She sulked, taking her hands from his flesh, rolling on her back and brushing his groping hand away with a certain amount of petulance.

"Shit!" He sat up in the bed and stared at the small window with its thin curtains doing nothing to hide a view of brick wall beyond.

"Joe..."

"Wot?"

"Don't you love me?"

"Yeah!"

"You're a rotten bastard. All you want is what I let you have every Tuesday."

"You enjoy it, too!"

"Sure I do – 'cause you're shovin' it into me!"

Joe felt a sudden flow of energy. "Want it now?"

She took his hand and placed it on him. "No! If you're feeling horny, work it off yourself!"

"S'truth," he panted, feeling over her nakedness. "This ain't my week..."

"Joe... don't do that unless you want to..."

"Wot?"

She whimpered. "That..."

He crawled down the bed, down... kissing her sides, her hip, her stomach.

"Oh, God – Joe... Joe..."

His hands lifted her buttocks. His mouth wandered over each thigh, down to the knee, back to the inner tenderness of the thighs and his hands kept opening the thighs, wider... wider...

So intent were they on their lovemaking, they couldn't hear the slam of the front door, the heavy footfalls of Sally's mother as she approached her daughter's bedroom.

At forty-seven, Mrs. Morris looked, and acted, like a woman ten years older. The harsh war years had taken a deadly toll; and the constant battle to provide for a growing family had sapped all ambition. She existed now, for her infrequent shopping trips to Ilford and Romford; for the tea with gossip when she visited her sister in Barking; for the once monthly night at the pictures. She no longer fought her husband for her rights nor did she care what Sally did. She had tried with the girl – tried desperately hard to make her have respect for herself and stay away from that awful Joe Hawkins.

Today, she didn't feel good. The migraine had begun almost the second she entered Ilford and increased steadily until she had been forced to abandon her shopping and return home. She didn't like the frequency with which these blinding headaches struck; yet she did not want to see her doctor. She had a fear of medical men – a carry over from the war when she witnessed an on-the-spot amputation in a shelter.

As she slowly climbed the narrow stairs to her bedroom she paused, frowning. The sounds coming from Sally's room were suspiciously like those associated with passionate lovemaking. She listened, forcing herself to ignore the migraine for those vital moments...

"Oh, God..." She hurried now, moaning softly, hands shaking as she turned the bedroom door knob.

She closed her eyes tightly against the sight confronting her. "Sally! God, no!" A black sheet of pain covered her head. She clung to the swinging door for support, unable to watch their cavortings.

Sally couldn't stop herself. She was at the peak of her orgasm. Her eyes rolled open, and fixed on her mother's face...

She wanted to yell; to draw away from her lover and hide beneath the rumpled covers.

For the first time in her young life, Sally Morris felt sorrow for her mother...

"Yes... yes... yes..." Joe's panted exhortation beat on her ears, his body a pistoning battering ram pressing her down in the creaking bed.

The physical sensations blew away her shame.

And then, it was over; and the dregs of passion ebbed into an ocean of remorse as she struggled free of Joe's weight and covered her nakedness.

"Wot's the big idea?" Joe asked testily.

She pointed, silently accusing.

Joe glanced over his shoulder and felt a flush of hatred. *How dare the old bitch come in on them!* he thought. *Tuesday was his day in this house!*

"Mum..." Sally grabbed a blanket, hid her nudity and ran to her mother. Tears rolled down her cheeks, matching those staining Mrs. Morris's face.

The woman brushed aside the hand on her wrist.

"Please, Mum... let me explain..."

"You little tramp! You slut!" The woman's eyes opened, staring wildly. "Get that bastard out of this room..."

Joe leapt to his feet. "You old cow..."

"Joe!" Sally swung round. "Don't call Mum names."

He paraded his naked, sweating flesh round the room, deliberately taunting both of them.

"Your father wasn't wrong about 'im..." Mrs. Morris groaned, pain lancing through her head. She leant against the wall as her legs turned to rubber.

"Make 'im leave, Sal..." she sobbed.

"Joe..." The girl pleaded with tearful eyes.

With an ugly grin, Joe began dressing, taking a perverted delight in their eyes watching him. He'd been satisfied with Sally's performance and now there was the bonus of knowing that her mother could not quite prevent herself peeping to see what he had to offer. Only when he had gratified himself did he leave them alone and walk downstairs to the front door. Before opening it, he paused and shouted: "When you want what Sally likes be sure an' let me know, Mrs. Morris..." Smiling, he slammed the door behind him, and walked to the nearest pub without one regret, without the slightest thought for Sally's predicament.

# CHAPTER TEN

WHENEVER Sergeant Jack Piper came home, his parents dipped deep into their meagre savings for a special meal. Nothing was too good for their soldier son, the Pipers always told neighbours – and they meant it too.

Jack knew the circumstances and felt a bastard when he sat down to a perfectly-cooked meal with all the trimmings. But, he never complained, never spoke to his mother and requested a smaller tribute. He just fitted in with her plans and then, the day he returned to base, he slipped his father whatever he could afford to replenish the family coffers. Usually, it worked out well for the old couple. Jack was a decent son. Having a jar with the boys was always secondary to seeing that mum and dad had enough to exist upon. No matter what part of the world he was serving in, Jack always managed to send a parcel home.

Jack Piper loathed the district his parents insisted on making their home. He had been glad to join the Army just to get away from the rows of houses, the smoke-belching factories, the dirt-littered streets and the old-before-their-time people with their sad faces. He had never been able to understand why his dad wanted to stay put in the old, semi-slum home. His dad had been somebody in the Queen's Army in Africa and India – a colour-sergeant possessing medals and ribbons galore.

"Do you still follow the Hammers?" his dad asked.

Jack laughed. "When I can. They ain't doing too good lately."

"Give 'em time, son," The old soldier suggested placidly. "They're a young team. One of these days we'll be on top of the First Division."

Jack lit a cigarette and held his lighter out for his dad to place his worn pipe against the flame. He didn't want to discuss West Ham's chances of ever again topping the Division. He frankly had grown away from the local team, preferring to lend his support to an Army match down in Aldershot. "Found many winners over the sticks?" he asked, tactfully switching subjects.

Charles Piper glanced in the direction of the kitchen before answering. He knew that Madge knew he had the occasional flutter on the nags but he didn't like voicing the information in her hearing. They had long ago reached an understanding on his betting, and his visit to the local. What she didn't know didn't cause friction in the house. Each of them went along without ever mentioning the small win, the quick nip, the Saturday night dart game where stout and companionship compensated for all that was vastly different from the old days.

Jack grinned. He was a good-looking man in his late thirties. When his wife said he looked like a youthful Cary Grant when he grinned she was not far wrong. Of course, he wished he had the star's money. He would be able to afford a decent home for his parents, a plush flat for his wife and a private-school education for his two kids. For himself, he would buy a Rover car, a small cabin-cruiser, a retreat far away from the London filth and his freedom from the Army. Not that he found much wrong with an Army career. The forces had treated him generously and he had no valid complaints – except one... he didn't enjoy the unnecessary bull when some big shot decided to visit the camp.

The ancient features cracked into a smile. "I've had my wins, son. A tanner each way treble is good enough for me."

*God*, Jack thought, *they still take tanner bets down here.* "Anything worth betting on today?"

Charles Piper puffed contentedly on his briar, gazing into the fire. "Could be Mister Piercer will give them all a shock," he said with accumulated wisdom. "He's been running in low-class company. I say he's been held back for today's big race."

Jack grinned at a dancing devil in the fire. "Ten bob each way, eh?"

His father looked up, startled. "That's a lot of money to wager, son."

"I can afford it, Dad. Fact is, I'd like to split the proceeds – call it a father and son bet, eh?"

The old man shrugged. He loved his son, and the respect that a man his age expected from an offspring. He wondered how many men his age in this area could get the feeling of parental love that they shared. Not many, he guessed. Not many!

"I'm not certain about the horse, son..."

"I am, Dad! Agreed it's a fifty-fifty proposition?"

"Agreed, lad," Charles Piper said, hiding the tears which threatened to spoil the gesture.

"Which bookie do you normally use?"

"Dick Hedley."

"What time is the race?"

"Three o'clock."

"Right – soon's Mum has dinner served we'll shoot down and make the bet."

"Jack..." Watery eyes surveyed the son.

"Forget it, Dad! Values have changed, that's all. Tanners are fine for old age pensioners but we're paid pretty good money in the Army today."

His mother stepped into the room. She had heard the conversation and decided it was time to rescue her husband from an overly-emotional experience. "If you gentlemen will excuse the cook," she laughed, "dinner is ready. I'm afraid it's only bangers and mash but can guarantee the sausages are the best in London."

"Just what the doctor ordered," Jack said with a smile. Embracing his mother he added, "You remember how I love bangers..."

She shook her head. "No, tell me, son."

Entering the kitchen, Jack wanted to cry on his mother's shoulder. Grandma's best china was on the table and heaped mash on his plate was probably what they both took during any given week of his absence. The six sizzling sausages for him and the three for each of them had broken the Post Office account. "It's fantastic, Mum," he said with a gulp. "I feel like a general..."

His mother laughed. "Get away with you, Jack Piper. Your generals eat caviar and smoked salmon and sirloin steaks. I remember once when Dad and I were in India and Sir John Clacksley came to the mess for dinner. He had a dozen oysters, a pheasant, soup, a Bombay duck and sweet with black coffee. And do you know what he said about the dinner afterwards?"

Jack shrugged. "What?"

"He said, 'Why is it always a sparse meal when one is entertained in India?'"

Jack gazed at the table before him. "I think Sir John was a bloody bore! This meal is fit for a Prince of Wales and I don't give a damn if Wales like sausages or not."

Jack Piper didn't pay much attention to the coal delivery men when they interrupted the meal. His father went to attend to the necessary arrangements for removing the wooden slat they had across the coal bunker and came back to finish his meal. Then, when the knock sounded, Jack leant back and waited until his father settled the bill, unconsciously adding this amount to what he would give the old man when he finally went back to his unit.

He half-heard his father's quavering voice contest the cost of coal, and figured it for another increase the old man hadn't heard about until...

*"Pay up or else, you old bastard..."*

Jack stiffened. In this district people addressed one another with what amounted to blasphemy, he knew. But this... He jumped to his feet, marched stiffly to the back door and stared at the cocky kid with a coal sack over one shoulder.

"Or else what?" he asked.

Joe Hawkins glared at the stranger. He hadn't expected the old couple to have visitors – certainly not one wearing the uniform of an army sergeant, "'E's refusin' to pay up," he said defiantly.

"Jack – look at this…" Charles Piper held out the altered bill to his son.

Jack took one fast look and laughed. "Sonny – your arithmetic is haywire. This says five times sixteen bob is five quid. That isn't right."

"Look, mister," Joe snarled, refusing to back-pedal. "I collect wot it says on the bill. I want five nicker or else."

"Or else what?" Jack said softly.

"I takes the coal back, is wot," Joe snarled, again.

"You'll leave it where it is," Jack said. "I'll phone the office…"

"You'll fuck off!" Joe shouted.

Jack studied the bill closely now. He sighed. "Seems this has been altered."

Joe tensed. He could handle old age pensioners but a soldier… those boots matched his for effect! "Do you want bovver?"

"Yeah, sonny," Jack said, smiling coldly.

Joe didn't hesitate. His right foot lashed out seeking a vulnerable spot.

Jack Piper grinned, catching the foot, flipping the rest of Joe on his back. It was so simple when one took into account all those experienced instructors who trained men in the art of self-defence.

Joe came to his feet, caution forgotten. He had always made an extra quid at this house and he didn't want any clever soldier to spoil his untaxed income. He shot forward, hands slashing air, feet trying to find a solid groin to dig into... finding only a hard fist to the jaw, a knife-edged hand to the Adam's Apple and a boot in the bollocks to send him gasping amongst the newly-delivered coal.

"Tell the office to send the bill by post," The soldier growled. "If it's right we'll pay. If it isn't we'll take it up with the accountant."

As Joe struggled to climb off the shifting coals, Jack Piper guided his father back into the house, and locked the door in Joe's face.

All the fury of his encounter burst like a bomb inside Joe's mind. He had been relegated to an inferior position and this riled him; more – it positively went against his grain. He wanted to make the bastard pay for the indignity of being sent on his arse in the coal; for being shown to fabricate delivery slips.

Shaking his fist at the Piper house, Joe swore: "You'll pay for this, you bastard!" He glowered at Jack's grinning face in the kitchen window and stomped off to berate his mate for not coming to his side in a time of extreme peril...

# CHAPTER ELEVEN

"'Im an' 'is mates," Joe concluded as he fondled his latest weapon – an ancient, rusted iron bar with sharp teeth serrating one edge. No doubt it had once been a gear-activator, a sliding set of teeth to regulate an obsolete device.

"It don't pay to bash-up soldiers," Don remarked more to himself than Joe.

"'Ere," Billy interrupted with sudden enthusiasm, "did you read the paper tonight?"

Joe studied his closest confederate, wondering what bright-eyed inspiration was forthcoming. One could never tell about Billy. He read every edition of the *Standard* – practically devoured each word a dozen times over – and although most of the articles and news went way over his head, he did have a knack for recounting specific items by heart.

"They arrested Ronnie Goodman larst night!"

Joe was aware of a tightening in his chest, a butterflying sensation deep in his stomach. "And?" he asked eagerly.

"Six months!" Billy said proudly.

The tightness developed into a steel band round Joe's chest. He could hardly breathe.

"'Is mob..."

Joe snapped, "'Is mob needs a new leader!"

Billy grinned. "Yeah!"

"I know Hymie Goldschmidt," Don offered.

"Ronnie's lieutenant," Billy cut in.

"Christ," Joe barked, "don't I know it, too!" He waved aside Don's open mouth and allowed wonderful thoughts to trickle through his mind. If Goodman had been put away for six months he might just be able to swing the command of his mob. It would take diplomacy; no single group of skinheads ever willingly joined forces with another yet... they were both West Ham supporters and both lots came from Plaistow. It may not be so difficult...

"Don, find Hymie an' arsk if he'll talk to me."

Billy rubbed his hands gleefully. "Cor, mate — won't it be sumfin' if'n we can get 'em in with us?"

Joe stared at his pal. How the hell *he* ever read so much and spoke so badly was a mystery. Even Joe felt he had a better command of the Queen's English than Billy. "You're a cunt..." he flung at Billy.

The youth grinned. "That means I'm useful, eh Joe?"

Ignoring the standard remark, Joe swung on Don. "Find Hymie. Tell 'im I want a meeting."

"Wot about the soldier?"

Joe smiled evily. "If Hymie an' Ronnie's mob join us we can beat the 'ell out of that bastard!"

*

Hymie Goldschmidt was a Jew. His father owned an empire of rag-trade outlets near Aldgate and they lived as his grandfather had lived in Prussia – in squalor conditions. He refused to belong to his native nation – preferring, always, to sponsor the Israeli cause and plough his gains into bonds for a foreign country. He did not sympathize with his English relatives nor would he ever bend a knee to accept the dogma that England, as a Christian land, could have anything he wanted... unless, of course, one took into account the plentiful supply of cash in this God-forbidden island. In all his business dealings, Solly Goldschmidt acted on the belief that an Englishman was a sucker and that the Jew-boy was supreme when it came to making money. He spent very little on family luxuries, accepting Council charity in the form of a home subsidised by the non-Kosher ratepayers, and devalued the worth of the security he had by possessing a British passport.

Where Solly was Orthodox, Hymie said "to hell with all that crap" and – when his father was working – helped himself to large ham sandwiches, bacon and eggs and anything else he figured would drive his mother insane. Many a time his grandmother scrubbed out their refrigerator to cleanse it after Hymie had deliberately insinuated ham into its Kosher depths.

As for Israel – well, Hymie must surely have been on the "most wanted" lists of their Secret Service. He hated Israel with Arabian loathing; he cursed the day Palestine had been handed over to "those European misfits" and offered proof that "no evidence existed to back the Jewish claims to the occupied territories they now controlled."

Hymie was, to all his friends, a non-Jew; a dis-believer; a semi-Christian. He even went to the extent of attending Mass with some of his mates or looking in on a service in St. Paul's Cathedral whenever arguments at home drove him to emphasise his Anglicized nationality. Occasionally, when the Rabbi forced him, Hymie would attend his Synagogue – but always under protest and always dragged by his father.

In a household dedicated to the accumulation of money and subjected to the belief that the Jews were God's "chosen children" – which he denied fervently – Hymie was, without any doubt, the greatest throwback in history. He was intelligent – knew every aspect of British history; could place spots on a global blank map with the accuracy of a Marco Polo; quote from Burns, Shelley, Wilde and Keats; argue politics and religion with great authority; bedazzle accountants with a natural Jewish flair for profits-versus-overheads.

Yet, notwithstanding, Hymie was also a skinhead – a violent little thug devoting his energies to the dismemberment of those who professed to love, adore and understand.

When Ronnie Goodman was sentenced to six months Hymie believed he could assume command of the mob. Believed...

His ego was shattered when the mob refused to obey his leadership edicts. He felt betrayed.

When Don came to see him, Hymie was more than willing to throw-in his lot with yet another Gentile commander and reassess his situation. He didn't make his feelings evident; he always hid his thoughts.

"Alright," he told Don, "Joe Hawkins has a name – but is he capable of leading a big mob?"

Don glared at the Jew. Personally, he could have chopped the hook-nosed bastard to bits but he remembered how Joe would have acted. He forced a smile, and said, "Sure he can! Arsk any-one in Plaistow."

Hymie mentally agreed that Joe Hawkins had a name. There were enough people running scared to make him a suitable stand-in for Ronnie. Anyway, he wanted to set up a situation that would be resolved when Ronnie came out of prison. He wanted to watch the two leaders fight it out for supremacy. If either, or hopefully both, flopped then – maybe – he stood a chance of assuming ultimate command.

"We have twenty-five in our mob – how many are in yours?"

Don hesitated. Hymie knew, like everyone, the exact count. He tried to get around the issue. "That's not the point..."

"How many?" Hymie insisted sadistically. He had already decided to enlist the support of as many adherents as possible but he still had to place Don, and through him that bastard Joe Hawkins, on a spot.

"Seven..."

"Just seven?"

Don tried to make sense of his mental fingers. His worst subject at school had always arithmetic.

"Fifteen..."

Hymie ignored the difference. He liked Don although he knew the other hated his guts. That, he told himself, came from the East Ender's inherent belief that all Jews were bloodsucking moneylenders and slave-employers... a fact he could not deny without bringing in statistics to show that there were others – Gentiles – equally guilty of the same charge.

"Where is Joe?"

Don beamed success. "I'll take you to 'im..."

Hymie laughed inwardly. Dropped Hs spoke of servility and inferiority in his book. He went with Don...

*

"Alright," Hymie said. "We join mobs!"

Joe smiled. He didn't particularly like the Jew-boy but he did respect Hymie's abilities and his promise to bring Ronnie's mob in with his.

He thought of that bastard Piper.

"Look, mate," he told Hymie, "we're goin' to visit a house near 'ere tonight. I want a soldier done..."

"That's fine with us, Joe," the Jew replied non-chalantly.

"Bring your boys to the..." he thought, then said, "Greengage at seven-thirty eh?"

"Right!" Hymie shook hands, sealing the bargain. It was official now – Joe's mob had grown into a force worthy of his leadership.

*

Jack Piper got from his comfortable chair and glanced at his mother. She was snoozing, head propped on hands to make it appear she was interested in the television programme. Jack smiled, shook her, and said, "Mum – go to bed. It's an awful show."

The old woman shook herself awake, trying to smile. "I'm sorry, son..."

"Don't be, mum – go to bed. Dad's asleep too." He motioned to his father who was curled in his end of the sofa with eyes tight shut and snores gently issuing from compressed lips.

"He's a silly old B," Mrs. Piper said lovingly. "Can't stand these late shows, he can't."

Jack grinned. It was not quite nine-thirty and he knew their need for sleep. "Mum, I'm going to the boozer. I've got a key so why don't you and dad go to bed?"

"What about your supper when you come in, son?"

"Mum..." He placed an arm round her shoulder, helping her to her feet. "Forget that! I'm not a child now. I can make something to eat when I come home..."

"You're sure?" she asked with a true mother's feeling every son was absolutely helpless.

"I'm sure, mum. The army taught me to fend for myself."

She laughed, throwing her arms around him. "Jack..." she sighed. "Jack... you're a wonderful boy!" She kissed his cheek, then eyed her husband. "Isn't he a soppy date?"

They shook the old man awake and helped him upstairs. Jack knew that the Scotch – Teacher's from the off-licence – had taken its toll. His father wasn't used to a treat and, especially, for six glasses neat. Jack had wondered about the amount consumed. He believed in the Teacher's edict: Moderation has its rewards... or words to that effect. He didn't knock Teacher's Scotch whisky. He firmly held it as a friend of mankind. Providing one always held to the code of moderation, nothing gave such a feeling of well-being and relaxation as a good old Teacher's did. For himself, he never drank Scotch unless the label had the distinctive name on it.

When his father was safely in bed and his mother preparing to climb in beside him, Jack slipped from the house. Walking down the street, Jack felt that familiar desire to set fire to the slum properties. In his estimation – after seeing some of the places the army had to offer in far-flung regions of the globe – this district was sadly in need of an arsonist's expertise. He couldn't stand the run-down factories, the shops with their cheap goods, the overall impression of poverty and low income buying.

He was feeling in a bitter mood as he reached the local. He didn't honestly wish to enter. It was always the same these days when he came home on leave. He felt so bloody sorry for the old men sitting around the lonely bar. It wasn't too bad for the dockers and the Ford workers. They got a bloody good screw. But the pensioners – shit! he thought savagely, they've been robbed of decency begging to a Welfare system that demands they queue in sterile, unfriendly offices and go down on bended knee to some supercilious Civil Servant who only knows the rule-book method of handling people. Men like his dad who fought for their country didn't deserve to be treated as names in a book, rubber stamps on triplicate forms. They were men, and women. Solid people. The honest backbone of Britain. They deserved much better than a socialist free-for-all and begging for supplementary benefits.

"God help us all," he said aloud as he went in.

"Wotcher, mate," a hefty labourer laughed as he entered. "Christ, you get talkin' to yourself an' they carts you orf!"

Jack grinned, slapping the man on the shoulder. "Sorry, chum – I was thinking about me dad."

"S'alright me son," the other cried, "'ave a beer on me."

"Ta," Jack nodded, shoving through the normal door-jam crowd.

"Beer fer me mate, Rosy," The man shouted to the Irish barmaid.

"Make that Teacher's and soda... I'll pay the difference," Jack said hurriedly.

The Irishwoman shrugged, causing her monstrous breasts to do a jig inside her sweater. She didn't mind his eyes feasting on them. In fact, she repeated the gesture to give him a second eyeful before smiling her way to the bottles. Jack hid his amusement. It never paid to take the mickey out of an Irish barmaid. The regulars didn't like it.

"Ain't you Jack Piper... Charlie Piper's lad?"

Jack turned slowly. The old man facing him presented a toothless smile and an outstretched hand. He nodded, accepting the friendly shake.

"Cor, I remembers you when you was a nipper," the man said. "An' look at you now..." He studied Jack with an admiring gaze. As the barmaid deposited Jack's drink the old man eyed it speculatively. "Lemme buy it, son," he said without an effort to reach for his pocket.

Jack grinned. "Have one on me, mister." He handed Rosey ten bob.

"Scotch?" the quavering voice asked.

"Scotch for the gent, Rosy."

"Bless you, son. T'ain't often we gets the chance..." He halted, conscious of his *faux pas*.

"Forget it," Jack smiled. His drink tasted perfect and he handed a cigarette to the old man.

"Where's Charlie?"

"In bed... where you should be!"

The man laughed, bending to light his cigarette from Jack's butane Ronson. "Son," he explained, "I sleep till noon so's can spend every night in 'ere."

"It can't be much fun..."

"No," The old face grew serious. "These young yobbos make it hard on the likes of me. They don't 'ave respect no more."

"Do you play darts?"

"Me eyes ain't wot they was, son..." and when he saw Jack's sudden disinterest he quickly added, "but I could give you fifty up?"

"We'll start from scratch," Jack said. "Come on... let's have a game."

*

For an old man, the friend of Charlie Piper certainly threw a mean dart. He wasn't kidding when he offered Jack fifty-up. Playing for beers (and Jack was glad it wasn't Scotch) cost him a few bob. He didn't win a single game and when another couple of pensioners joined in for a foursome it still cost Jack his cash. After all, he reasoned, he was the worst player on the board and he didn't expect his mistakes to come out of a paltry allowance.

Walking home, he felt the evening had had its compensations. He had renewed his faith in a dying breed – the old soldiers of London.

He didn't have a chance. They came at him from every angle. With iron bars, broken bottles, steel-toed boots and chains. They swarmed over him, knocking him to the ground, kicking and gouging and slashing with all the ferocity of their ugly minds.

He couldn't recall much of what happened. He knew he'd been hit with something hard; something solid; something brutally unyielding. And, as blood spurted to blind him, he felt the waves of them pour over him...

# CHAPTER TWELVE

"His condition is extremely serious, Sergeant."

From where he stood, Sgt. Snow could see the bandages, the ugly bruises. He was used to violence and broken bodies, just as Dr. MacConaghy was accustomed to making running repairs to them.

"Have you any idea who did this?"

The sergeant shook his head angrily. "Not by name, doctor. We know it was a bunch of skinheads and that's all."

"Skinheads! My God – can't our society control even them?"

Sgt. Snow stiffened. He didn't want to listen to a tirade about the ineffectualness of the police; nor did he have the inclination to have his role in the investigation questioned.

"Sorry, Sergeant," the doctor smiled wistfully. "I'm not condemning you and the force..."

Snow smiled easily now.

"I'd just like to know where it's all going to end," MacConaghy finished.

Snow didn't reply. One didn't make an issue of problems when one wore a uniform; regulations formed a tight noose round a man's tongue and political solutions were left to those chasing votes. Stricter controls over demonstrators, over students who forgot that the public paid for their right to education, over skinheads at football matches and on special trains were definitely required. Stiffer penalties would help too.

The doctor made notations on Piper's chart, swung away with distant eyes surveying the stained, grime-coated exterior of the hospital as seen from a small window. "Same outlook for a man trying to recover body and soul, eh, Sergeant?" he murmured.

Snow studied the view. He found it repulsive, sickening, and was forced to agree with the doctor this was, indeed, the worst possible sight for a recuperative patient to watch. "Even a high-rise block would look better," he said slowly.

"There's half the trouble," the doctor remarked. "Environment! Can one blame people living in that for wanting something different in their dreary lives? The youngsters see it and remember it. They think of areas where other people live –

Belgrave Square, Richmond, Surrey stockbroker belts where the grass grows green and a man can look around him and see just merrye olde England's glorious land."

"You're saying then that crime is directly linked to the slums?"

"Sergeant, when it comes to crime I'm a rank amateur," the doctor grinned. "I couldn't steal a purse from a cripple." He scowled. "That was bad taste! Seriously, though, I'd like to see what a dictator could do in this country. Slums wiped out, harsh measures to curb the grab-all boys, savage sentences for injury to persons, hanging for child rapists and cop killers, the birch for young offenders like these skinheads."

"Pretty effective penalties," Snow laughed as they progressed down a dismal corridor.

"Since when does molly-coddling criminals pay dividends?"

Snow refused to be drawn. He accepted the doctor's remark; could have enlarged on it. But again regulations stopped him.

"Get yourself an iron bar, Sergeant," MacConaghy suggested as they reached reception. "The next time one of those young thugs starts making noises, break his head. I'll have the pleasure then of sewing him so it hurts." He held out a hand. "I'm supposed to cure ailments and heal people but, just once, I'd like to slice away the evil parts some of these kids have in their heads."

Snow shook hands solemnly. He understood the doctor's feelings. Patching up cracked skulls wasn't funny. No more than seeing a damned good soldier stretched out flat because some of the kids he constantly defended against totalitarianism had decided to make mince-meat of him.

"When you've had a go at the little bastards bring them here, Sergeant."

"I will, sir," Snow smiled thinly.

Both of them knew it would never happen. The British policeman was allowed the private thoughts of his fellow-countrymen only in the seclusion of his home. Outside those walls he was a machine – ordained into an order totally against counter-violence. And for that reason alone, he should have been protected against those he tried to apprehend...

His Thursday showed a profit of £2-15-0. His body ached but that twenty five minutes with Mrs. Scalatti had softened the pain. There was something about Maltese women that made him feel the itch. At forty, the Scalatti woman was going to fat but he didn't care. He enjoyed meat on them; and, as he told Billy that evening – "I bounced on her like an aircushion!"

"The paper says that soldier is 'overing close to death," Billy remarked, ignoring Joe's daily tale of birds screwed on the job. Billy was worried. He didn't mind the occasional punch-up, the aggro with other skinheads, the sadistic beatings they gave to hippies and the hard battles against the Hell's Angels' crowd. That was part and parcel of his life – why he wore skinhead gear and fashioned tools from the workshop at Ford's. But he didn't like kicking a soldier until he was nearly dead. He had a respect for soldiers – his dad had been one as were his brothers Tom and Eddie.

"Serves 'im bleedin' right!" Joe snarled viciously. He wished to hell the bastard had kicked the bucket. He'd never forget the indignity of landing on his arse.

"Christ, Joe – if 'e dies..."

"So wot? They don't know we did it!"

"I don't like it," Billy voiced, hands deep in pockets, kicking a tin-can into the gutter with a savagery that belied his concern.

"Fuck the soldier," Joe snarled. "I'm thirsty. Let's 'ave a beer, mate."

The pub was almost empty. The pensioners had already taken their pitiful allotment home after a beer and chat. The dockers and their wives wouldn't be here for another hour yet and those layabouts who drew Social Security to keep their booze intake at a steady level were probably at the dogtrack.

As Joe and Billy entered, the landlord hurriedly sent Mary in search of unwanted spirits. He didn't want his pub mentioned in the *News of the World* as the location of a scandalous affair.

"Two pints," Joe ordered, watching Mary vanish down-stairs. He still liked the idea of them all ganging her. When they got her he'd have first go… and last too.

"There's a dance in Ilford tonight," Billy said, equally enamoured with Mary's swinging cheeks as she disappeared from sight.

"So wot?"

"So there's birds an' Pakistanis galore…"

Joe tensed. Pakistanis! "Where?"

"Hymie knows…"

"An' where's Hymie?"

"Right here, Joe. Make that three pints, guv…" came a sudden voice.

Joe didn't turn. He forked out the extra, then asked, "You always creep up on a friend?"

Hymie laughed. "I was here before you came in."

"An' where's the dance?"

"Are we going to be there?"

"Bloody right!"

"Abraham – move over. Hymie is coming to fuck a little hot bitch of a Jewish bird!"

Joe grinned. He liked this Jew-boy. All the stories he had heard about Jews and their continual search for money and Gentile birds meant nothing when it came to Hymie.

"You know, Joe," Hymie declared enthusiastically, "I've been trying to get this cow to drop her knickers for months. Her old man is a friend of mine and she won't say yes in case I put a bun in her oven. Moses, how stupid can she be! I always carry five French-letters!"

He quickly opened his wallet, displaying the Durex. "Anyway the way she rabbits around with that bloody Catholic Mike Kallinan she should be pregnant!"

"The soldier is nearly dead," Billy said, still wrapped up in his private worry.

Hymie chuckled delightedly. "So what?"

"So the fuzz will be lookin' for us."

"Mate, we weren't there," Hymie said. "I've got friends in Notting Hill will swear we were attending a party there."

"Notting Hill?" Billy cried. "Christ – that's miles away."

"Exactly," Hymie smiled knowingly. "Relax, Billy – that bastard won't kick the bucket."

"I bleedin' well hope not!" Billy said seriously.

Eric Wilson often wondered what made him turn a successful gambling hall into a teenage dance hall. He knew one reason was the way the heavies had moved in and installed their croupiers and gaming machines; he remembered the day that a certain known boxer had calmly walked through the door and announced he and his mate were now partners in the club. Wilson had been unable to combat the mob and reluctantly agreed to sign papers to that effect. His choice had been simple – sign or have the club wrecked.

Until the new gaming laws had come into force he had been forced to sit back – a manager in name only – and watch the steady downfall of what had begun as an elite establishment. He had seen characters he hated become regulars; seen the standard of play vanish into a crooked table catering to an eighty percent profit for the house; seen old customers tail off until they no longer felt it wise to buck the odds.

And then, when the new laws were passed, he had been thrown on the scrap-heap of unprofitability. The boxer had moved into fresh ventures not subject to strict control, and he was left with a shambles of a club – unsupported by the locals, avoided by the criminal element, shunned by those who would drink in a friendly atmosphere.

It was at that stage he decided to interest the teenage element and started the dances. He hired local groups hoping to play enough reggae to appease the aggro boys.

But now, he operated a veritable powder-keg of teenage violence. Every night, as he opened the doors, he wondered what had been so marvellous about his original idea and why he risked neck and limb for the few pence he made each week. Damages alone cost him a fortune; even his huge Alsatian refused to act as Gestapo regulator after having his beautiful hide burned by cigarettes. A dog is a dog and after being savaged by thirty or forty raging teenage lunatics the Alsatian had decided that discretion was the better part of valour.

Thursday night was generally quiet. Most of the yobbos got paid on Friday. Most of the skinhead element came to gawk on Saturday. Most of the problems and the police visits were confined to Sunday when nobody else catered for a growing menace.

Seated at the bar with Bill Thompson, a reporter, Eric felt reasonably secure. A girl in a slash-fronted dress played a fruit-machine; a man with a permanent leer trying to date her sat nursing a large Scotch and offered suggestions as the female levered the machine's handle.

"You were a damned fool ever allowing the mob in," Thompson said.

Wilson recalled the fateful night when his club was invaded, taken over, and sent in a tailspin plunge to hell.

"And you're a worse fool letting these layabouts hold their tribal dances here."

Wilson shrugged. "Bill, you're so smart you tell me how I'm supposed to get my money back from the investment if I don't cater to the money crowd."

"Teenagers?"

"Yeah, teenagers. They've got the dough today."

"And what about Mr. and Mrs. wanting a night out? Don't they rate?"

"Shit!" Eric exploded vehemently. "They spend a few quid and expect Savoy service. This is Ilford, mate – not Mayfair!"

The two men sat silent, watching the girl on the fruit-machine go through the antics of a gambling maniac. She wasn't in the least bit interested in the leering spectator. She had one thought – the urge to hit the jackpot. That it was, legally, limited to pay-out didn't stop her insatiable desire for a win. It was the gamble that attracted.

"One of these days..." Thompson said softly.

"She's terrible," Wilson confided. "I've had it – all pull a handle and no push a coin in her slot."

A group of boys suddenly burst through the front door. From his stool, Eric Wilson surveyed their gear and moaned. "Skinheads!"

Thompson tensed. Even the girl on the fruit-machine hesitated as she sank another sixpence in the slot and held the handle with grim determination.

"Telephone the police," Thompson suggested.

"Why? They haven't done anything yet..."

Thompson shrugged. "Not yet."

"Bill..."

"Thank you and goodnight," the reporter said finishing his drink. Waving to the girl on the machine, waving to the lecherous man seated by her side, waving to Eric, his friend, he left hurriedly.

At the front door he paused, glancing into the dance hall. He could see the first signs of trouble – skinheads pushing to get the birds they desired onto the dancefloor. He felt sorry for Eric Wilson.

"Where's the Jewish bird?" Joe asked, conscious of a mounting desire to find something that somebody else wanted. From what he could see in the club, he didn't much fancy getting his trousers down.

Hymie said, "At the fruit-machine, Joe."

"Let's have it off, then..."

Eric Wilson watched as he saw the trouble develop. He knew, instinctively, that Joe and Hymie were only interested in Ruth. And, also, he knew she was only interested in the machine.

"Hiya, doll," Hymie said in his best Brooklynese-American. He liked affecting the accent, especially around Jewish birds.

Ruth ignored him, dropping another tanner into the machine.

"Look, chick..."

She jacked the handle then glared at him. "Get lost, you creep!" she snarled.

"Skip the machine," he told her warningly. "We're going to dance."

She fixed him with a hot eye. "Like hell we are!"

The machine clicked through its series, and spat out five coins. Her hand reached for them, but halted as Hymie grabbed her wrist. "Baby doll, we're dancing and then..." he leered.

"I don't enjoy it when they've been circumcised," she said hurtfully.

"This one you will," Hymie threatened.

"I'm not circumcised," Joe said.

Ruth glanced at him. "So, wank..."

Joe lashed out, catching her across the face with an open palm.

"Just a bloody minute..." Eric yelled, coming off his stool.

Joe swung, hand streaking for his tool... coming out with a knife.

Eric froze.

Afterwards, Eric swore nothing would have happened if the girl hadn't screamed. She pushed past Joe, darting for the door with Hymie in hot pursuit. The scene scared Joe and he lunged, ramming the knife into Eric's thigh, his face flushed, his eyes bulging.

In the club, the noise attracted attention. Like automatons, the mob erupted... slashing, kicking, hitting.

From his corner, Frank White watched the battle progress. He wasn't involved... not yet. The fix he'd had before coming here left him immune to all happenings – his was a joyous scene on its own.

A boy charged forward, knocked off-balance. His knife glinted evily, his face taut with emotion.

Frank rose swiftly – faster than normal. He zipped a gun from his shirt, fired without hesitation, seeing his victim collapse on the floor as if it was all a dream; a cinemascope technicolor extravaganza to equal that last epic he'd watched in Piccadilly Circus...

*

Sgt. Snow studied the chart. Even he could see that the graph was down. The kid had a bullet in his chest, dangerously close to his heart. Only top-doctoring could save him and even then it was doubtful if he would live more than a few days.

"You can speak to him, Sergeant," MacConaghy said. "He's conscious."

Snow studied the pale features. "Are you sure?"

MacConaghy shrugged. "Might as well get information while you can. He'll live – or die, depending on how we perform."

Snow felt sick. He couldn't understand the doctor's callousness. "It might lower his chances," he said.

"Like hell it will!" came the sharp reply. "He's on borrowed time now. Go ahead."

*

Roy Hawkins relaxed with shoes off, feet up on a small coffee table. The programme was interesting; an interview with Jack Dash on his retirement. Roy thrilled to the man's statements – especially those connected with a hardcore reserve left behind to look after the docker's interests in Jack's absence. He enjoyed the reference to containerization. He didn't like it any more than his mates did. He could see the system vanishing as new container ports grew in prominence. Falmouth first, then maybe such places as Scotland and Northern Ireland and Wales. No self-respecting Londoner would want work going to those areas, when, by right, it should stay in London.

Roy was feeling pleased. Not only was his ideal man being allowed to prove his abilities, but the trade figures again gave Labour an edge.

He heard the urgent knocking, ignoring it until his wife said, "Answer that, Roy!"

He knew Sgt. Snow. He grinned, stood aside, and said, "Come in, Sergeant."

Snow couldn't get used to warm welcomes with their cold-cold farewells. He preferred the suspicious half-open door, the growling display of indifference when he produced a search warrant, the laughing goodbye when he found nothing.

"They've got Jack Dash on telly," Roy said eagerly, leaving the door open wide for Constable Cheeseman to follow him inside.

"Is Joe in?" Snow asked.

Roy hesitated, then closed the living room door. His face was tight, worried. "What 'as he done?"

"A boy was shot tonight," Snow replied. "We think Joe was the leader of the gang that caused the trouble."

Roy opened the door and shouted: "Joe... come here!"

Sergeant Snow watched the boy saunter to meet them. *A right cocky bastard!* he thought.

"What?" Joe asked, deliberately avoiding Snow's gaze.

"Joe Hawkins," the sergeant said slowly, "I have reason to believe you took part in a shooting to-night..."

"That's a lie!" Joe snapped.

Snow smiled. "Perhaps you could account for your movements, son?"

"I was home all night. Arsk Dad..."

Roy felt guilty immediately. He stared at the floor, saw a spot the missus hadn't polished and murmured, "That's right, Sergeant."

Snow wanted to shout, "Mr. Hawkins... Roy... don't cover for him..."

Roy met the sergeant's gaze then. "Cover for Joe?"

Snow shrugged, told his constable, "There's nothing we can do here..." and marched down the short path to the pavement.

"Joe, I want the truth..."

Joe laughed. "You didn't take that cunt seriously, did you?"

Roy's hand flashed, knocking Joe to his bed. "I like Desmond Snow," he said.

"Then take 'im to bed!" his son screamed.

Roy smiled easily. He didn't believe in violence, nor sadism. But, tonight, he would teach Joe a late lesson. His hand lashed out again and again... each punch a telling blow... each a lesson in itself. More than once he hoped Joe's manhood would assert itself and force the boy to hit back. It never did – and the beating continued until Joe lolled around on the bed in a semi-conscious state. Only then did Roy Hawkins stop. He just hoped his wife had not heard the beating nor guessed that her son was as good as a murderer.

# CHAPTER THIRTEEN

Nobody could have called Joe's week a raving success. From the failure to see the match the previous Saturday until last night Joe had suffered more than he gave out. He didn't enjoy looking back down the days; it was just one of those best forgotten periods in his young life. Yet, he couldn't forget. Sergeant Snow especially had to be remembered. Joe did not take kindly to his father's punishment and blamed Snow for bringing trouble into an otherwise tolerable house. Until now, his antics had been overlooked but he felt positive they would no longer receive his father's indifference. Once aroused, Roy Hawkins could be an unrelenting, authoritarian foe.

All day, as he worked his fiddles, Joe schemed revenge on Snow. He wanted to have the mob batter him but he knew this was a delicate matter requiring no more than three trusted mates. Once the fuzz started asking questions Joe wanted to be absolutely certain that the weak links were already eliminated. Normally he allowed his desire for violence and publicity to overshadow any fear of legal restraint. But what he planned was not normal. One didn't do a copper every day of the week – even such a terrible week as this!

What he needed, Joe thought, was a solid alibi. If only there was somewhere the mob could attack...

He laughed aloud. His driver mate glanced at him suspiciously. "Wot's the joke, Joe?"

Joe waved away the query, concentrating on private laughs now. During the next four calls he didn't even try to fiddle. He wanted a perfectly clear head free from other distractions. He did the job with a speed that surprised the hell out of his mate. And, he did not speak to the flighty bird in 17... an unheard of feat.

When he jumped from the lorry as it entered the coal-yard, Joe had his scheme worked out. He was whistling when he entered his own home and washed, changed and left without once speaking to his anxious mother. For all her many faults, Mrs. Hawkins worried about her son. She would not hesitate to belt him around the ears nor did she believe he was a plaster saint. Yet, she was his mother – and the maternal instinct did beat faintly within her. She knew something terrible had happened and knew too that Roy had unleashed his fury on the lad. But no more. And it grieved her to be completely ignored just as she was on the verge of displaying some tenderness and understanding. It never struck her that the offer would be years too late. No more than it struck Roy at work that his thrashing had been delayed to the point of uselessness.

*

"Right, mates, 'ere's wot I want..."

Hymie, Billy and Don leant forward, conscious of Joe's low voice and the need for secrecy. Around them, disinterested men drank and argued about the next West Ham match. Behind the bar, Mary watched Billy – hoping for an opportunity to catch his eye and make arrangements for another meeting.

"Hymie – you get your lot an' 'ave 'em at Ilford station by eight o'clock."

"Right, Joe."

"Billy – chat up Mary. Tell 'er you'll meet 'er tonight when they close 'ere."

Billy grinned. "No bovver there, Joe." He began to rise.

"Sit down, you stupid bastard," Joe growled. As Billy sank into his chair with a frown, Joe explained, "We've got to 'ave everything worked out first."

"Wot about me?" Don asked rebelliously.

"You, mate, can find all the lads you can. 'Ave 'em at Ilford same time as Hymie."

Joe sipped his pint, settled back with the air of a general about to outline a highly dangerous mission behind enemy lines. Planning confidence showed on his face when he spoke again.

"Now 'ere's wot we do..."

Hymie listened avidly, feeling excitement course through him as Joe continued to elaborate. He liked the step-by-step daring of the plot; the underlying sensation of crowding in a week's bovver into one night. Tomorrow's Upton Park lark would seem tame after this, he thought fleetingly.

Billy did not have Hymie's imagination. He enjoyed some aspects of Joe's grand plan and especially where they would finish the night having a real old bang at Mary. But he did not like the most important part. He felt scared — and refused to voice his fear. His position as Joe's best mate was at stake and all the doubts in the world would not jeopardize that.

Don was neither excited nor frightened. He looked on the scheme as just another aggro — one with more risks attached but still an aggro. He nodded as each step was unfolded and when Joe ended his instructions he got to his feet, drank the remaining dregs of his beer and announced: "I'll round up the lads now."

From his chair, Joe watched Billy approach Mary, saw the woman's eyes fasten on the youth and smiled as she nodded a furtive agreement.

"That's that," Joe remarked. "Get lost, Hymie."

The Jewish boy slapped his thigh. "Mate, it'll be a fantastic aggro."

*

Arthur Mason wished he had refused the offer of help. At the time, it had seemed a wise course to count on a few dozen dedicated fighters but not now in light of recent developments. What should have been a refuge for homeless students was, in reality, an armed camp controlled by uncouth, sex-crazy Hell's Angels. And, what hurt most was the sad fact that squatters had no rights inside the building they had commandeered.

"Can't we get them out?" Tony Maxwell asked.

The bearded student shook his head as the frustration became an overpowering urge to smash things. "How the hell can we?" He flung his few belongings across the dirty floor. "Once they discovered the pot they took over."

From downstairs the sound of an orgy filled their ears. Arthur knew exactly what was happening; he didn't require a guide book around this place. They would be naked or partially dressed and the toughs would be having their fun before departing for yet another night. The bitches! he thought angrily. "Cheap tramps! Doesn't it ever strike them as degrading to have those bastards crawl all over them?"

Toni shrugged. She was a pretty girl, an intelligent girl. At twenty-four she considered herself the den mother of the house; a position she had abruptly surrendered when the other girls started acting stupid. "Is there a difference between men when all one wants is intercourse?" she countered. She could remember her own experiences with pot. She had not cared how she was used, nor by whom, nor how often providing the pleasures were fast and furious and the activity continued until her senses could stand no more. She didn't blame the girls for begging the Hell's Angels boys to make love to them; in fact, she considered all their unwanted visitors as strapping, virile men capable of sustaining sexual delight far beyond the capabilities of the male students. The outsiders didn't have the intelligent inventiveness of the more sophisticated students but how did one compare positional gratification when one was seething in convulsive passion!

"Oh, shit!" Mason snarled, digging into his jeans. "I'm not going to worry about them!" He drew a thin cigarette from his pocket, looked at Toni. "Want to?"

She nodded eagerly. "If you think it's safe..."

"There are sixteen girls down there – almost two for each of the others. Even they aren't supermen. No, it's safe enough!" He lit the joint, drew deep of its relaxing qualities.

"I don't want this bra torn," Toni said with a grin, remembering the last session and how impatient Arthur had been to fondle her breasts. She reached under, behind her sloppy sweater and unhooked the brassiere.

Toni accepted the joint and smoked it reflectively. As far back as she could recall she had delved in the mysteries of the occult. It was this addiction that had opened doors for other mysteries – sex and revolutionary movements and, then, pot. She wished, at times, she could slam the door just as that man had closed out interference a few seconds ago. Since becoming more involved with her demonstrator friends, she had not been given the opportunity to think things out for herself. She was caught up in a world of anti-everythings in the going-nowhere merry-go-round of pseudo-politics and, worse, the ecstatic mayhem that was surely destroying her body. Knowing this did not limit her writhing attendance on the physical side of "intellectual" companionship. Sex was, for her, an outlet; a means to prove she was above society and the dogma of the Church. It was a justifiable excuse for parading and defying authority; for committing herself completely to ideals which had already ruined her family link.

Inarticulate mouthings seeped through the wall, followed by frenetic bangings.

"Man, I hate those crummy bastards!"

She forced herself to return to the room, the lonely emptiness of sleeping bags and scattered clothing and the scrawled notations some of their companions had considered as decoration...

SEX – NOT GOD!
DOWN WITH AMERICAN PIGS!
LOVE THY NEIGHBOUR'S WIFE!
CASTR(O)ATE IMPERIALIST SWINE!

"What did you say, Arthur?"

He turned to her, leaning against her pliable softness.

His beard tickled, rubbing on her face, his tongue probing hotly into her willing mouth. His hand pushed aside the brassiere and cupped her breasts.

Over his shoulder, as he pressed her back down on the hard floorboards, she saw the scribbled red letters accusing her...

IT'S ONLY GOOD IF IT'S HARD!

She reached for him, hoping it would be good...
Constable Greenwood consulted his watch. Another fifty minutes and he'd be off-duty. He was sorry for the squatters but he didn't consider it a policeman's lot to mount guard over those breaking

the law. Frankly, in his opinion, the force would be better off letting all the warring factions fight it out and then swoop on the weakened remains. His wife had a more profound suggestion… "Give them guns and maybe we can all sleep in our beds after they wipe one another out" was her idea.

As he walked back and forth, Greenwood studied the nice houses along York Road. He had lived in Ilford all his life and this area – outside of the Cranbrook Road where the properties were elite – had seemed to him the perfect area for retirement. Since the war, though, there had been a steady movement away from private ownership.

The road had changed drastically of late. What had been residential and tranquil was becoming a hive of transient parasites swarming in, moving out, doing nothing for the community except create problems galore for the authorities. He did not blame landlords for making a profit where they could; he did blame them for excessive rents, and an uncritical examination of those they accepted as tenants. A little more time spent asking questions, checking references and some thought to the district as an integral whole could save the police hours of wasted manpower chasing those who skipped out with rented television sets, unpaid bills and stolen furnishings.

From outside, he could see people moving back and forth in the house. *Damned shame!* he thought. *I can imagine how they'll leave it...*

His heart hammered. Coming down the road – like a small army knowing it has superior firepower and unafraid of the opposing force – a bunch of skinheads leaped and pranced as they studied the houses.

*This is what the sergeant warned us about!* were Greenwood's first thoughts. Then... *Christ, I can't be expected to make this lot behave!*

He moved to block the entrance, face set tight, hand hovering over his truncheon. He would have to use it. There was no mistaking the mood of the invaders – nor the target.

Joe wanted to do a war-dance when he saw the lone constable stationed outside the squatters' abode. He had reckoned on at least four fuzz guarding the hippies. This would be a walk-over!

"Nevermind the fuzz," he yelled to his minions. "Charge!"

Swarming as wasps goaded into anger, the skinhead brigade surged forward, brushing aside Greenwood's lonely resistance. In an instant, weight of numbers battered down the front door, smashed windows, and raced round to the back in an effort to prevent the enemy from retreating.

Joe was in the vanguard as the skinheads ploughed aside the lightweight barricades the squatters had erected; still heading his men when they entered a reception room.

"Christ..." A huge, hulking brute wearing a leather jacket emblazoned with the Hell's Angel motif leapt to his feet, confronting Joe.

For the first time, Joe felt his intelligence had been faulty. Nobody had warned him to expect trouble from Hell's Angels. He knew, of course, that Piccadilly had been swarming with the skinhead foes but this wasn't Piccadilly; nor even a place a thinking Angel would expect a skinhead attack. What had gone wrong?

Joe lashed out instinctively. His tool caught the Angel across the face – slicing through to the bone. As blood spurted, Joe kicked – finding the groin with a devastating boot. The Angel slumped to the floor, battered into unconsciousness by angry skinheads.

From a corner, the girl watched the mayhem without seeming to care. Her nudity attracted one of Joe's mob and before she could realise her partner had changed, she was thrashing under a new lover.

Joe was distantly aware of the rape; very conscious of the Hell's Angels coming at them from every part of the house. He did not know how many of them were inside; he only cared about the rest of his plan.

"Find Hymie and let's get out of 'ere!" he snarled at Don as they battled back to the front door.

For minutes, neither could move — they were trapped by the mob trying to enter the house and by the Angels attacking with their chains and lead pipes. Even the students had joined their protectors and were driving the mob back... back... always back.

Constable Greenwood had a broken left arm. The agony of it sent blinding flashes across his eyes yet he mustered his strength to reach for his walkie-talkie. Another thirty-five minutes remained before his relief showed. Too long! They'd be killing one another in there if the battle lasted just five more minutes. He had to summon help — had to!

*

Sgt. Snow came from the hospital feeling like hell. He had seldom seen such seething pools of accusation as he had when he gazed into Piper's eyes. The soldier would be fine — after a month's treatment. That helped give Snow hope but he would not easily forget how Piper had silently blamed him, and the Force, for his injuries.

From what Piper had said, Snow knew Joe Hawkins was mixed up in the brutal beating. But could he prove it? He wanted to, very much!

Walking home, Snow reviewed the situation. Joe had tried to cheat Piper's father and the soldier had shamed the lad by knocking him down. That alone justified revenge in Joe's language. Then, the attack. It was all too pat for mere coincidence. It had to be Joe. Maybe if...

At the next corner he changed direction. He entered the local police station just as the news broke – a skinhead assault on Ilford squatters had resulted in a constable being injured and in several combatants going to hospital. One of the skinheads – a lad of fifteen – was in critical condition. He had been stabbed in the stomach. And, he lived in East Ham...

Sgt. Snow chewed his lower lip. Could this be the break he wanted to crack Joe Hawkins? he wondered. If the skinhead came from this area and Joe was a leader of the mob then perhaps...

"Cobb... get me a car. I'm going to interview that kid..." he roared. Quickly, he arranged to co-operate with the Ilford station. He couldn't just rush in when it was outside his jurisdiction. He had to have permission and, considering the circumstances, this was quickly forthcoming. In less than fifteen minutes Sgt. Snow was being driven to Ilford district hospital...

# CHAPTER FOURTEEN

"THAT STUPID bastard Hymie..." Joe thought as Don, Billy and he waited in the shadows outside the hospital. All his carefully prepared plans down the drain of Hymie's rotten luck.

"Look, Joe!"

Joe followed Don's finger. He tensed. Even at this distance he could see the sergeant step from the police car and enter the lighted area of the hospital casualty department's door.

"Is he...?" Don started to ask.

"That, mate," Joe said harshly, forgetting that Don's concern was for their companion, "is the bastard I want done!"

Billy shivered. "Not tonight, Joe. Christ – Hymie's..."

"Hymie's a fuckin' Jew an' can take care of 'im-self." Joe edged an inch closer to the huge gates guarding the hospital precincts. "'Ey, 'is car's leavin'..." He wanted to shout so great was the joy inside him then.

"Ah, Joe – it's too dangerous," Don complained.

Joe swung on his mates. "It wasn't dangerous before Hymie got 'is, was it?"

"No – but..." Don spluttered into silence.

Billy wanted to run. Something was seriously wrong with Joe's mind if he imagined the three of them could take on a copper. Those bastards were *trained* to fight dirty!

"'ow about you, Billy mate?"

Billy bit his tongue and said nothing. His face showed the extent of his fear but he steadfastly re-fused to go against Joe.

"Right, it's settled. When 'e leaves we do 'im!"

*

From his vantage point across the busy street, Da-vid Sansome watched the furtive prowlings of the three boys. Half inclined to telephone the police he forced himself to wait. He did not like being a nui-sance, nor did he truthfully know why he felt they were acting suspiciously. He had heard the news bulletin and could understand that even skinheads and hippies must feel a certain sympathy for a wounded comrade. He told himself it was his vivid imagination that made the shadows flitting back and forth near the hospital seem so wrong.

Just in case he was failing in his duty to notify the authorities, though, he kept his precious camera by his side. If anything did happen he would have a visual recording of the events.

Considering that he only worked as a maintenance man with Ford's he had an expensive array of photographic equipment in the house. He was, plainly, a camera-bug. Every penny he could afford went into new darkroom materials and his successes were many in the amateur field. It had always been his ambition to be a Press photographer although necessity had long ago relegated him to exhibition work and the occasional "London's Day" type of picture in a newspaper.

The camera by his side had cost him £350; the telephoto lens another £125. He was proud of camera and lens and, especially, his latest venture into the field of infra-red photography. Using this equipment, with a highly sensitive film loaded, he could practically guarantee results.

And, now, watching the boys across the street, he was sure he could snap them doing whatever it was he feared they may do...

Sgt. Snow was dissatisfied with his results of his hospital visit. Hymie was in bad shape; certainly too weak to talk to anyone. The doctors had expressed concern at the amount of blood the boy had lost and they rated his chances of recovery at a low ten percent. According to one doctor, Hymie had been stabbed several times with a bayonet.

As he approached the hospital gates, Snow was vaguely aware of the three youths coming towards him. He didn't associate them with danger; why should he? – youths came to visit sick people like any other human being!

It wasn't until his arms were suddenly seized and twisted behind his back that he realised something was terribly wrong – and then it was too late. Far too late...

He felt the savage kick catch his jaw, and sagged.

He felt a second boot crash against his temple and the night became inky-black, enveloping him in swirling mists of pain and horror...

# CHAPTER FIFTEEN

Joe Hawkins sounded cheerful at breakfast. His Friday had more than compensated for all the disasters of the week. He had his revenge and nobody would ever be able to point the finger of guilt at him. The vision of Sgt Snow returned, as it had all night, to please him. Looking at his mother's idea of bacon and eggs made him think anew of Snow – bleeding and battered, insensible and unable to identify his attackers. They had been careful; so bleedin' cautious.

Roy Hawkins entered the kitchen, face unshaved, hair uncombed. Rubbing sleep from his eyes he studied Joe's Cheshire face, and asked gruffly, "Wot's up with you?"

Joe stuffed bacon in his mouth, washed it down with insipid tea and got to his feet. "There's a pop concert in Hyde Park today."

"Wot about the football match?"

"Stuff that!" Joe replied lightly. Nothing could get him down today. Just nothing!

"You young 'uns." Roy shook his head sadly as if the world would end when a supporter would miss a West Ham game for any bloody concert. He swung to his wife. "The trouble is 'e thinks there won't be any bovver is wot 'e thinks!"

Joe shrugged and opened the door. "Jesus, dad – grow up! It's the first free concert of the year... I ain't goin' to miss that!"

As his son vanished, Roy stared at the unpalatable mess on his breakfast plate and shoved it aside. "I'm not hungry, dear," he offered as an excuse, wondering if Barney would have a decent meal at the corner caff. After years of his wife cooking Roy had reached a compromise stage – he feigned a weak stomach and ate out whenever possible.

In his room, Joe dressed with all the ritual of a soldier going on parade for a visiting brass. He couldn't tell the mob what a big man he was, not yet. Not until after the fuzz dropped their enquiries into Snow's beating. But he still felt tops. *It wasn't every skinhead done a sergeant, was it?* he asked his reflection in the mirror.

*

Outside the local, Billy darted from an alley and shoved the *Daily Express* at Joe. "Look at that!" he screamed, scared shitless as his trembling hands held the paper open.

Joe looked and felt instantly sick.

The picture carried the credit: *by David Sansome*. It showed Joe, Don and Billy in dramatic action as they attacked a beaten police sergeant.

"Christ, Joe – we've had it!" Billy wailed.

Joe couldn't hear Billy. He was struggling with the write-up:

### LAST SECONDS IN BRUTAL ATTACK ON POLICEMAN

Hardly had the camera shutter clicked than Sgt. Desmond Snow fell to the ground, yet another victim of skinhead thuggery.

Sgt. Snow was visiting a wounded victim of another skinhead encounter when he was suddenly seized and beaten into unconsciousness, a helpless victim of senseless viciousness. The frozen horror of this picture captures once again the problem of our times – The Youth Revolution. If we are to expect our policemen to give us protection we demand then surely it is our duty to stamp out this terrible evil that is threatening all of us.

No father, or mother, can feel proud of her son when viewed in the light of this attack.

But it is up to you – the parents – to assist the police in their efforts to put a name to the vicious thugs who perpetrated such an obscene crime...

*Where the hell had the photographer been and why hadn't they noticed the flash-gun?* Joe thought immediately. Nobody could mistake his face. Nobody! He was a marked man; a criminal on the run now.

"Joe... Joe, for God's sake say something!" Billy wailed.

Joe started to push open the pub door. "Let's go to Marble Arch."

"No, Joe – I ain't goin'," Billy said.

"Why not?"

"Joe, they'll clobber us for this!"

"So?"

"So, I'm not going near Hyde Park tooled, is wot."

"Ditch it... I won't."

"Joe, for God's sake, can't you unnerstand – I'm scared! That was a copper we done..."

"An' so?"

"An' so I'm not goin' with you!" Billy retreated two yards, hands ready to fend off any blow.

"You're yellow," Joe shouted.

"Bleedin' right I am," his mate confirmed. "Coppers don't like their sort bein' done. If they catch us, Joe..."

"They remember the rule-book wot says they can't hit a prisoner."

"Shit! Joe…"

"Where's Don?" Joe asked suspiciously, feeling lonely.

"'E's gone to the match…"

"An' the others?" Now Joe felt really alone.

"They backed out. 'Onest mate, I want to come with you but…"

Billy did a fine impression of a dummy being jerked off-stage. "I'm scared!"

"Wot a bloody mob," Joe snarled. "One picture in a fuckin' newspaper an' they turn yellow! To hell with you… I'm goin' to Hyde Park…" He swung away and stalked off.

*

On the Underground, Joe felt the loneliness of the Amazonian explorer; the feeling of departed civilisation; the glare of publicity that robs criminals of friends, neighbours, the sheltering crowds. At least, he reasoned, Hyde Park would shelter him from the spotlight. There would be so much going on nobody would want to concentrate on a single individual. After the show he would have a beer, a nosh, a chance to consider his future plans. He never considered the possibility of capture; the "he's not with us" ritual most of his type affected when confronted by law and order. He forgot the running scared streak down the back of every young thug – and old, for that matter – and the self-protective desire of underworld characters to save their own skins regardless. The code of honour that supposedly existed in criminal circles and was, again supposedly, relevant to skinheads, hippies, revolutionaries and Hell's Angels did not enter into his thinking. He placed his faith in his personal ability to avoid disaster; to apply the native fox-like cunning to any given situation.

By the time he reached Mile End the train was packed solid with teenagers going to the concert. He felt safer. His was a face that did not conflict with those around him. He had distinguishing characteristics and so did the others. Plus, of course, the fact that countless thousands would attend this special show. It wasn't every day that youth demanded its tribute to the revolution against society's strict codes on pot and LSD and free love. This was *the* protest to crush all opposed to youth's right to call the tune.

He was tooled but not in anticipation of bovver from hippies, Hell's Angels or any other youth cult. He was tooled because, naturally, this was a Saturday. No real skinhead ever ventured forth on a Saturday without his trusty weapon. None!

Today meant an extra few shillings for Constable Webster. He had no choice in whether or not he would give up a duty free Saturday.

If he had his way, Webster would have eliminated concerts such as the one taking place. He did not hold with policemen being forced to offer protective services to those ferociously dedicated to the total destruction of all that the policeman was forced to uphold. He did not take kindly to being shoved, pushed, called obscene names whilst smilingly upholding the peace of Her Majesty's lands.

"Move along, son," Webster said kindly.

"Fuck you, fuzz," came the short sharp reply.

Webster controlled his impulse to hit the young bastard. Instead, he laid a hand on the person's back and pushed. Gently, but firmly.

"'E's molestin' me," came the immediate retort as a scowling, antagonistic face was presented for the constable's provocation.

"I said – move along," the constable said again, minus the friendly tone.

The yobbo laughed, "'E's bein' nasty!"

A group of long-haired clipped-hair teenagers surrounded P.C. Webster. For a few ugly seconds he thought – *Lord, what have I done to deserve this?* – then, as a soulless sound burst from the microphones on-stage, he felt the mob melt away, surging towards their idols.

Like bad pennies rolling down a gutter, the mob rolled in a solid wave. Crowding, surging, flowing into an ever-packed mass. Closer, tighter, jammed into a mass that could not contain them...

Webster struggled to free himself of the crush – fighting to retain his official position on the *outside* of the gathering.

And then...

His jawline tightened, his hands itching to grab the young thug.

Joe felt the hand on his shoulder and figured it as another yobbo trying to get ahead of him. He wanted to be as near the platform as possible, wanting to hear the undistorted sound as it bathed him in ecstasy.

"Lemme go," he screamed above the raucous noise.

"Don't struggle, son... you're coming with me..."

The deep male voice stung Joe to action. He tried to whip his latest tool from its hiding place under his shirt... couldn't as the crowd grew tighter, less controlled. He glanced around, saw the helmet, the blue uniform.

"We wish to ask you certain questions, son..." The voice said in his ear.

Joe kicked... felt his boot strike a hapless shin, found himself in a strong grip...

In the lonely cell Joe felt the world was indeed a wonderful place. He had been questioned – without brutality. He had been identified by the photographer – although how he could see when he had been forced to use infra-red was a little beyond belief.

But it didn't matter, according to Joe's thinking processes. It didn't matter a bleedin' bit.

Once he paid his fine – which Social Security would fork over anyway once he pleaded "compassionate circumstances" – he would be free; free to continue as he always had; free to rule with an iron fist over *his* mob. None of them would dare question orders now. Not after he had made the big time by having his picture in the papers and being sentenced.

Oh, yes – Joe Hawkins had it made. He could go on to better things after this. He had been scared about how the fuzz would treat him but they'd been very correct – tea and sandwiches; questions without kicking him around; even a reporter allowed to get his viewpoint of the incident.

Somehow, he didn't mind missing the concert. Not when he was being given the full treatment. He didn't understand that a prisoner was innocent until proven guilty, of course. In Joe's book everyone was guilty of crimes against him until he kicked the shit out of them and forced them to assume positions of subservience. That was the difference between society and Joe Hawkins – and he probably never knew it existed. His was a senseless world of violence for the sake of violence; his ideal devised by those wishing the end of civilised behaviour patterns; his the starstruck era of pop and pot and the belief that might is right even if might has to play games and call itself right.

From today, Joe Hawkins was made. His name would rank with those others in the crime underworld. He had done a police sergeant and he would face the consequences – a fine, a warning, a beration and the all-essential publicity.

Oh, the stupid bastards – didn't they ever learn! Didn't they know that his crime being publicized would make him a king of skinheads!


THE END

# SUEDEHEAD

## (OPENING CHAPTERS)

# CHAPTER ONE

As HE STOOD in the dock, Joe Hawkins considered his situation with utter detachment. Legal procedures meant nothing to him. He had done a police sergeant and now he faced the consequences of that action. What *they* – those stupid bastards going through the motions of justice – did not know was how all this was making him an even greater figure in the eyes of his pals.

Joe listened to snatches of the case against him. He was not troubled about the outcome. It was always the same – a fine, a warning, publicity. He returned the magistrate's glare, he smiled cockily at the coppers in court. He refused to assume an innocent attitude. Nobody was going to say that

Joe Hawkins ever knuckled down to authority. He was a law unto himself.

Suddenly, Joe felt tension mounting inside him. The message reached his shocked brain. This wasn't any common or garden fine. Not the way that old buzzard was talking. This wasn't a warning to behave like other decent citizens. This was the big walk – bird...

"*...eighteen months...*"

Joe was stunned.

"*You may step down. Next case...*"

Stumbling from the box, Joe felt strong hands grab his arms. Realisation smashed into him like red-hot daggers probing for a vital spot. Eighteen days was a lifetime but months sounded like the total end of all his dreams. The gang would forget him in a few weeks. When he came out there would be nothing for him to command. Some rotten bastard would have taken control and he – the famous Joe Hawkins – would be a skinhead without mates.

"He can't..." Joe struggled. "He bloody can't do this!"

"That's where you're wrong," a harsh-voiced policeman said. "You've got off light. If I had my way..."

"Nobody arsked for your opinion," Joe snarled, striving desperately to keep his cool.

The policeman grinned and motioned for the others to remove this *object* from the courtroom.

He had no sympathies for those who deliberately attacked coppers. The magistrate had surprised them all with his treatment of Joe and, the bobby thought, *about time too.* Practically every member of the force believed that stiffer sentences would eliminate eighty percent of the injuries they sustained doing their duty.

Joe's co-ordination vanished as his legs turned into elastic. He felt weak, ready to scream. Half-dragged, half-staggering, he made it downstairs into the cells. According to one of the fuzz he had a short wait – and then…"Clobbered you, eh?" a thin-faced youth smirked as he picked at a sore on his ear. "I got three years."

Joe shuddered. "I expected a fine."

"That's the way it goes, mate. It all depends on how the beak's missus treated him the night before!"

"What did you do?" Joe asked unemotionally.

"Knifed my girl," came the easy reply. "The little bitch held out on me." Blood trickled down the ear and a dirty handkerchief was hurriedly used to stem the flow. "We had an agreement how much she would charge, then I discovered she was upping the ante and keeping the change." Narrowed eyes surveyed Joe's face. "You ever tried pimping?"

Joe's head shook a fast negative.

"Man, it's the life. They do all the work and you collect."

Something about the youth frightened Joe. Not a physical fear but a deeper menace which went against his grain. Not many things bothered Joe but pimps were scum and their treatment of girls they professed to care for left him cold.

"I once had a black chick..." The youth kept talking, evidently proud of his record. He was about Joe's age yet there was a worldly wisdom in those narrowed eyes which went with his thin, hungry, cunning face. Every so often he examined his blood soaked handkerchief and nodded.

Joe lost interest after the first few sentences. He had problems of his own and how this other prisoner had spent his freedom did not matter. Nothing mattered except those eighteen months inside. Could he take it? Could he emerge feeling like Joe Hawkins of old? Or would prison have a sapping effect on him? He knew several old lags near his home and hated to think he would ever look like them.

"...and you can have her address if you like."

Joe shook his mind awake. The youth had not noticed his preoccupation.

"Man, she's a terrific worker. Six, seven marks a night. That's money, man."

"I'll give it some thought," Joe said.

"Do that, mate. You'll be out long before me. I'm not going to get remission."

"Why not?"

The youth laughed. "I've done porridge before. I'm not worried about it. I like breaking every rule in their book."

*The hell with that! I'm going to get full remission*, Joe thought.

"Stick with me," the youth said softly, eyes wider and shimmering now. "I'll show you the ropes…"

*

Standing on the street with the Scrubs a gigantic horror behind him, Joe Hawkins took a gulp of air down into his starved lungs. It wasn't that this air tasted fresher, or had less pollution in it than the air breathed back there in Wormwood. It was just that here, on the outside looking in, there was a freedom quality he had been denied for far too long.

"You goin' my way Joe?" Nobby Clarke asked as he hefted his bundle under one ancient arm.

"Naw," Joe replied thankfully. He did not want to be seen anywhere near the old lag. It had been great finding somebody he knew by sight in prison but once outside he was determined to avoid all ex-cons like a plague.

"Lemme give you a tip, Joe," Nobby said brightly. "Never get nicked for anything small. Next time make sure they gets you for a big job!" The old man shuffled a few feet, turned and grinned. "Go see that woman I mentioned. She'll help a kid like you!" He winked and hurried off.

Alone now, Joe thought back to the first day of his bird. That had been bad but not nearly anything like when he discovered he was a special target of every queer in the Scrubs. God how he loathed those bastards! He had always figured homosexuals to be small, dancing men with carefully manicured hands, lisps and a walk that signposted their aversion to women. He had found that they did not belong to any such tight limitation. Some of the ones who had tried to lure him into their cells were big, strong, typical heavy types. One especially had been sent up for murder – a vicious ex-boxer with a protection racket backing his penchant for desirable young men.

The queers had been bad but they had not been the worst of his problems. Even now, after all that porridge, he could not get used to regimentation and loss of identity. The soul destroying routine had shattered his self-confidence until Mr. Thompson had seen fit to take Joe under his wing. In a sense, Joe felt a debt of gratitude to Thompson. As a screw he was a pretty good egg. But he was a screw! And although he had gained permission for Joe to take a course in office procedure, and got him a job in the prison administration section, there was that barrier – prisoner and screw!

Some of the old lags had been kind, tolerant of youthful mistakes, eager to pass along knowledge gained from years spent doing prison sentences. Nobby had been most helpful. Thanks to him Joe had managed to evade the dirtiest jobs and make sure his lapses weren't reported.

"Never again," Joe whispered to himself.

Far ahead, Nobby shuffled along – a lonely, beaten old man with but one thought gnawing on his saturated mind; back to Plaistow and the boozer. Joe didn't give Nobby more than a few weeks freedom. The man was beyond rehabilitation. He'd blow his bankroll, make a couple of visits to Social Security and then, when the boom was lowered, he'd do a sloppy job and get nicked again.

*Now take me*, Joe thought. *I'm young. I'm smart. I'm not going to commit a crime like Nobby. I've got an address and I can make out okay until I get a job. There'll be birds and booze, but not another visit to the Scrubs.*

Taking his time, Joe walked in Nobby's wake. He knew exactly where he was going. The magazine article had shown him the root. Skinheads were dead, man. Phased out. Home had never appealed. All his life he had dreamed about a plush flat somewhere in the West End. So now he would make the leap from poverty street into the affluent society. In one gigantic jump. The advice poured into his ears by all those old lags had taken root. If he was to succeed he had to plead, and beg, and make like a downtrodden slum-dweller whose environment had been the root cause of his imprisonment.

*They must be stupid*, he laughed silently as he began to whistle.

# CHAPTER TWO

Bernice Hale had known poverty as a child and this made her extremely susceptible to the pleas of those whose homes she could associate with her own background. When Joe Hawkins entered her pathetically small office she felt an immediate "relationship".

"Mrs. Hale?"

"Sit down, Joe. Relax. I'm here to help you – not scare the hell out of you!" She smiled and waved to a chair.

Joe sensed the desire to get on friendly terms. It was just as Nobby had said it would be. He sank into the chair and returned the woman's smile. After serving his porridge he needed to look at an attractive woman and think about some of the girls he had known before that old bastard of a magistrate handed him time.

"You've been a model prisoner," she said with blue eyes scanning the dossier.

He nodded, judging her to be around fifty. She was slender enough to be a movie queen and her vital statistics left nothing to be desired.

"I've a son your age," she said, fixing him with an expression that vaporised all his notions of an easy bit. "Being in prison sometimes makes a *man...*" and she stressed the man, "yearn for female company. I'd advise against hasty decisions, Joe. You're not in any position to spread kings yet."

"Nobby Clarke sent me to see you..."

"I have a dozen Nobby Clarkes on my books, Joe." She got to her feet and breathed in deeply. Her breasts thrust against a woollen jacket. Her eyes caught his, and air whooshed from her lungs. "That was silly wasn't it?"

He continued to stare.

"Joe – get those ideas out of your mind." She came around her desk, hitched her skirt and sat half on, half off the edge of the desk. Her stockinged legs enticed, provoked, sounded clarion calls in his frustrated mind. "I'm being a tease, I know. But then..."and she laughed huskily, "I always am."

He could not make head nor tail of her tactics. She seemed to be begging for him to make a move. Yet, was she? He did not dare risk it. He sat hard on his chair, perspiration beginning to roll down from his armpits.

"You pass!" she said briskly and extended a slender hand. "If you had made one move to assault me that would have been the end!" She shook his hand, and hurried back behind the desk. "I've a thing about sex maniacs. I don't like them!"

"I only came here to ask for help, Mrs. Hale."

"I take it that means money?"

Joe nodded. He was confused by her tactics.

"For a room?"

"Yes. I don't want to live at home."

"Why not?"

He shrugged. "Reasons..."

"Name a few!"

"I've been inside. I don't want to go back. My parents would crucify me."

"I see..." She consulted her file. "You were a vicious monster, Joe. Skinheads are, unfortunately, a product of our ultra-permissive society. Have you changed enough for me to trust you?"

"I can go to Social Security," Joe growled, getting to his feet. So much for Nobby's bright idea!

"Sit down!"

Joe felt compelled to obey. There was hidden strength in this woman.

"We don't sponsor habitual criminals," Mrs. Hale told him. "Our aim is to give the first offender an opportunity to establish a working relationship with his fellow men. We have a strict rule – help once, no more."

"I'm not going back," Joe replied sourly.

"I should hope not. How much money do you have?"

He emptied his pockets, placing the meagre amount on her desk. Glancing at the pathetic result of his prison pay-out, she smiled scathingly. "Not much for what you've suffered, eh?"

"They haven't got unions in prison yet," he answered with a sneer.

"That's quite enough cheek," she snapped. Counting his cash she said; "That's grocery money, Joe. I have an arrangement with a landlady in Islington. She'll provide a room and breakfast. It's not a palace but you'll have a front door key and freedom to come and go as you please. "

"Thanks!" He sounded bitter. Nobby had given him such glowing accounts of this outfit's cash reserves and how they treated their clients generously.

"Your attitude leaves much to be desired. I suppose your old lag friend spun you a yarn about how soft we were..." Her gorgeous breasts flattened on the desk as she leant forward. "Joe, pay attention to me."

His eyes fastened on her breasts. His pulse quickened. She was a magnificent woman and frustration seethed like super-charged electrons inside him. "I am," he said truthfully.

She ignored the obvious. "I'm going to tell you a story, Joe," she said evenly. "My son lives in Canada. He served five years in Kingston there and got a loan from this society. With it he met a girl, got married and found a job. Today, thank God, he's an honest citizen and owns his home, a business and has two beautiful children. That's why I work here, Joe. If my boy could do it – so can you." Joe sat motionless. *Why did they have to pour on the soft soap*, he asked himself. He didn't believe her. This was a standard approach to someone fresh out of stir.

"You've got doubts?"

He shrugged. "That's not for me to say."

She opened her desk drawer and pushed three scraps of paper across to him. It took less than five seconds for his eyes to confirm the truth of her tale. The newspaper clipping had the name Hale in bold headlines. The society loan agreement photostat showed that Hale had been granted five hundred dollars repayable over a set period. The third item was a glowing account of John Hale opening a community centre which his prosperous company had seen fit to build for the town's youth.

"Satisfied, Joe?"

He pushed the material back to her. "Yes!"

"My son never had a decent thought in his head until he served time," she said. "I despaired of him but now..." and her eyes moistened in motherly pride. "He's justified the faith I've placed in him. I'm a sentimental fool, Joe. I know this will shock you – and the society. I'm going to give you a chit for twenty pounds. I advise spending it wisely. Take ten and get roaring drunk. Find a girl and take her home with you. Relieve yourself. But don't make a habit of it. Mrs. Malloy does not like her bathroom occupied by strange women every morning."

Joe felt strangely touched. This was against everything he had considered possible. He wanted the money. He wanted the society behind him. If his plans were ever to reach fruition stage he had to have the backing of a solid community agency. But Mrs. Hale was putting trust in him. Placing him in an invidious position. If he failed her... He mentally rejected her wiles. What the hell! He was Joe Hawkins. Not a Hale. This stupid game was meant to soften him. He would not yield.

"Try to better yourself, Joe" the woman said, writing the chit for his cash advance. "I believe there is good in everybody. I hope you won't let me down."

He accepted the chit and smiled. "I won't, Mrs. Hale."

Outside her office he breathed deeply. So much for that! The woman was a sucker for a hard luck story. Once his twenty vanished he could come back and beg for more. He would have a story to tell – all sobs and under-the-skin frustration!

*

Mrs. Malloy was short, fat and ugly. She spoke with a thick Dublin accent, and smelt of wash-tub detergent. Rubbing clean, almost raw hands on her apron, she stood in the doorway studying Joe as he eyed his room with candid disgust.

"Bhoyo," the Irish woman said, "forget your grand notions. This is Islington and the Society are paying for your keep. Back in the Auld Sod there are fine fellas wishing they could afford such luxuries. Take my Uncle Sean..." She sighed as if trying to find someone to do just that! "He lives in me mother's auld house with its roof falling in and the rats climbing into bed at night just to get warmth."

"Where's the loo?" Joe asked.

"A fine thing..." She said "thing" like it had no "h". "You're everything Mrs. Hale said you'd be." Her ugly features showed contempt. "You'll be wanting a key, no doubt?" She walked to the window, fluffed curtains to hide the solid brick wall a mere three feet away. A thin shaft of light edged into the narrow confines of Joe's "home" and served to highlight the shabby furnishings. "I'm Catholic," the woman said stridently. "I'm agin mortal sinning but Mrs. Hale knows better than I..." She shrugged as if to state where Mrs. Hale stood in her estimation. "There's an awful lot of terrible diseases in London today."

Joe grinned. The old biddy was trying to warn him against bringing home an "unclean" girl! Looking at her he wondered if any man had ever managed to get close to her soft-centre. She was roly-poly in a most nauseous way. A man would have to be blind, drunk, desperate or very insensitive to take this one to bed.

"Patrick Kelly shares the toilet with you. He lives in the next room. You'll be wanting to meet the dear boy..."

*Not me*, Joe thought. *I'm not going to get tied-in with a bunch of booze artists from construction sites.*

He knew all about the Irish labouring types and how they roamed the streets before the pubs opened and how they sang their "rebel" songs with a skinful of booze making each and every one of them imagine they could wipe the floor with all English inhabitants after the pubs closed. More than once his gang had waylaid a lone Irishman and beat the hell out of him. Just for kicks. Just to even the score, as Benny had once said.

"If my husband was still alive – bless his soul – he'd tell you a few truths," Mrs. Malloy remarked, retreating to the corridor outside Joe's room. "He spent sixteen years in prison!" She got uglier as frowns creased her blubbery face. "What a rascal he was, Joe... broke heads like skittles in an alley, he did. There wasn't a copper could tame my Mick."

"Charming," Joe allowed.

The woman scowled which only served to heighten her bushy eyebrows and those hard lines near her mouth. A discerning individual would have understood the terrible hardships which had produced such an unattractive female. Not Joe, though. He was filled with self-pity, and other people's problems washed off his uncaring hide.

Taking a Yale key from her apron, Mrs. Malloy said: "Breakfast is at seven-fifteen sharp."

"Seven-fifteen?" Joe wailed. Looking frantically around the sparse room he asked, "Where do I cook?"

"Not in here! You can use the kitchen anytime after twelve noon if you have to eat in. My other bhoyos don't do that." She sounded anxious to put him off cooking.

"I was told..."

"Mrs. Hale doesn't live here," the woman said firmly. "She's a lady. I'm not. Nor are my guests gentlemen." The point was made and she relented briefly with a quick smile.

Joe kept his retort to himself. It pleased him to have one thin-edge to wedge in Mrs. Hale's door. He could always complain that his cash did not stress to restaurant or cafe meals. Any excuse was valid under the circumstances. He could not continue to live in this worse mousetrap which Mrs. Malloy called a room. It was ten times more horrible than his room at home in Plaistow – and that was bad enough.

"I'll be looking for a job," Joe said, changing subjects. "In the city," he stressed emphatically. "I'll want a key to the post box..." He could see that locked cage attached to the letterbox downstairs.

"You'll get your letters at breakfast," the woman said menacingly.

"Why can't I have a key?"

Hands on wide hips she snapped: "'Cos nobody but me is allowed to sort the post. I don't tru..." She stopped and swung abruptly.

"You don't trust jailbirds," Joe finished.

She hesitated momentarily, and then continued down the corridor as if afraid to pursue this line of questioning.

*What a bloody mess*, Joe thought angrily. *It's as bad as prison. I'm trapped with nowhere to go!*

Closing his door, Joe examined the dingy room in detail. That brick wall hemmed him in as effectively as bars on a window. The tatty covers on the sagging bed were below standard issue even for the Scrubs. As for the small chest of drawers, the wardrobe and one tilted chair, they had come from Noah's Ark and had been junk before an elephant sat on the chair or tigers sharpened their tearing claws on the other two items. A threadbare carpet from an Honest Ed's bargain basement did little to cover dry rot floors. Wallpaper that was so faded to have lost its distinctive floral design completed the picture of misery.

"Chrissakes, this is hell!" Joe yelled at that brick wall.

The touch of folding money in his pocket drained some of his hate. Then, he swore aloud again. What woman, or girl, or even club hostess would come back to this... this... this stink-hole of an abode? He hurried to the bed and pressed down on its wilted mattress. The rusting groan of battered springs sent their squeaking lullaby through the house.

"That's bloody it!" Joe shouted. Rage boiled up inside him and he kicked the chair. Splintering wood confirmed his fears. It had been an *impossible* seat anyway!

Thrusting arms into his jacket, he stormed from the room. His feet sounded like tanks rumbling down an incline formed of loose shell. He tore past a startled Mrs. Malloy and slammed the front door. Anger made him unaware of the pretty girl in hot pants brushing past him as she fumbled for a key in her Indian-style fringed handbag. He could only visualise Mrs. Hale and hear her remark: "It's not a palace..." *Bloody right it isn't*, he thought. *It's a tragedy – a free prison for ex-cons to discover how society gave to those who had repaid their debts!*

*

"Here's your bloody money back," Joe snarled as the twenty quid skittered across her desk. A fiver floated on an isolated air-current and drifted unheeled to the office floor.

Bernice Hale smiled grimly. In all her experience she had never encountered such an irate young man nor had money thrown at her. Usually they came in with their hats in hand and begging in their weak eyes. But not Joe Hawkins. He was strong stuff.

"When you make out a report be sure and mention this," Joe growled, beginning to turn away.

"There won't be any report, Joe."

He halted in mid-step, stared at the woman facing him across the paper-littered desk.

"What is wrong, Joe?"

He leant on her desk, face twisted into a contorted mask of frustration. "Mrs. Malloy is an Irish pig and expects everybody to act like she was giving them the world on a silver platter."

Bernice smiled generously. "That's not bad for you, Joe," she said softly. "Your kind don't normally stoop to poetic expression."

"You're making a bloody fool of me," Joe rasped.

"I am not! Perhaps you haven't stopped to examine what changes prison has worked inside your mind, Joe. Perhaps you always had a brain which could cope with the finer things your environment did not encourage. Perhaps not. Anyway, your choice of words strike me as being a notch above those skinheads I have the dubious pleasure of assisting."

"I'm not a skinhead now," Joe said, remembering his determination to disassociate with a former existence. He had to play his cards with masterly skill. He could not relax one single second in front of this woman. So much depended on getting accepted; established in an organised society to which she belonged.

"You were one of the best..." and she laughed lightly, adding, "or worst."

"I was," Joe affirmed proudly.

"And?"

"I'm not going to stay at Mrs. Malloy's!"

"Why not?"

"God," he exploded, "Have you seen that dump?"

"Is it that bad?" she brushed a paperclip which had attached itself from a blouse button. His gaze automatically fastened on her breasts. Self-consciously she covered her treasure chest with a file.

Joe got the message. *She's bashful after all,* he thought. *She's a tease who can't go beyond a certain set point. Once a guy gets the upper hand she's putty.*

Bernice Hale quivered inwardly. She hoped Joe Hawkins had not noticed her infantile attempt to turn his masculine frustrations away from those abundant charms which, she knew only too well, excited less deprived males. In a way she detested her wonderful bosom. It was a target for lasciviousness, for speculation, for passes she did not want made. She could not, however, deny herself the pleasure of mental seduction. She was all woman. All female as Eve would have it. And in the knowledge of the exquisite power her chest measurements gave her she basked in either glory or torment.

Joe calculated his chances. She was more than twice his age but he'd heard that the old ones were the best. Who was it who'd said: They don't yell, they don't tell and by jove they don't swell? Could he make the grade? Or would that ruin his ambitions?

He decided to play safe and ignored those hormones demanding he capitalise on the woman's confusion.

"I'd rather be in jail than stay in that room, Mrs. Hale," he said with a measure of truth which lent sincerity to his voice.

Thankful for small mercies, Bernice Hale breathed easier and placed the file back on her desk. The moment of indecision had departed on

Adam-strength wings. Or the ones he wore before the apple was eaten! "I haven't personally visited Mrs. Malloy's establishment," she admitted. "One of my colleagues gave it a recommendation."

"He didn't look at *my* room."

"Nor have the experience of what happens to a man once those prison gates shut, eh?" She smiled to relax his tenseness. "Joe, tell me honestly – what did you dislike about Mrs. Malloy's place?"

He considered her question. The native cunning which had taken him to the top of a skinhead gang and brought him to that fragile pinnacle of success for those fleeting hours of glory came rushing to his rescue. He was totally incapable of matching intellectual fencing but he knew when to duck and weave once fists started to fly. And this was street warfare. He was the underdog, the underprivileged. She the power, the rich, the one able to take away or give freely.

"I'm trying to get a decent job, Mrs. Hale. I need an address managers will respect. I need some comforts if I am to work my way to the top – not broken chairs and a bed that belongs in a dump."

She nodded thoughtfully. "Can you find a place yourself?"

"Yes!" He shouted the word, anxious now.

"I'm going to go overboard for you, Joe," she said falteringly, not quite satisfied with her decision yet realising it was all she could do under the given circumstances. "I'll advance you a loan. You'll have to sign for it though," she added pointedly.

"That's okay, Mrs. Hale. I'll refund it when I get work." He would have promised the moon plus a shilling for cash.

"Mark my words, Joe – this is your lot. Blow the cash and you're out in the cold."

"I won't let you down, Mrs. Hale," Joe said with mental fingers crossed she wouldn't change her mind at this stage.

She drew a chit across the desk, glanced at his face before writing figures. She could not know that Joe Hawkins was an actor. That the face he presented for her approval was but a facade behind which woodworm worked its nefarious quest.

"Sign here, Joe."

Catching himself in the nick of time, Joe scrawled his brash signature. Fifty quid! No interest. No repayment date. Just a name and the money was his...

"Let me know where you are staying," she said softly. "I'll want to visit you there."

He killed a thrill. If she came to his room he'd try her, for sure. Mother-age or not, she was everything a virile hunk of manhood dreamed about. He had seen her in a dozen erotic nights as moonlight filtered through those prison bars. Her, or a thousand panting females of all ages, all colours, all sizes. His face withheld the untold pleasures his mind conjured up and he kept his voice level as he said: "Thanks Mrs. Hale. I won't let you down."

"You said that once before." She laughed, handing him the initialled chit. "Joe Hawkins, you're a challenge for me. You're so like my son…" Tears moistened her eyes. She forced herself to regain control. "Remember where he went once he discovered that people are not all bad. Good luck in your job, Joe…" Her hand reached out and she stood – an attractive woman in her prime – as the lusting young man standing on the threshold of life let her warmth briefly touch his hard, unyielding, unsympathetic palm.

9 781911 095415